THE THIRD MOUNTAIN

6/15/20

To Meridy

- with all my love forever

Babe
Janette

READERS' REVIEWS

Dear Rabbi Freundlich,

I very much enjoyed reading the essays in your latest book, *A Cup of Gladness,* and I thought it was a very fine contribution to my own thinking and the way in which I would like to demonstrate the beauty of Judaism.

I am amazed at how prolific you are as a rabbi and as a writer. May God give you the strength and vitality to be able to continue to illuminate the lives of your readers, friends and admirers.

Very cordially yours,

Rabbi Haskel Lookstein, New York

"I have read every one of Rabbi Freundlich's books which are a collection of short stories poignant for the reader who is Jewish and the reader who is not, but who enjoys stories which highlight human joys and foibles. This book by the author may be my favorite. The stories are imbued with authenticity such as rivals within the rabbinate, childhood friendships, theological debates within different branches of Judaism, the difficulty of being a Jew in a smaller community and intra-synagogue debates. I not only admire his personal integrity and commitment to "honest" Judaism as a religion and culture, but I also greatly admire his style of writing which resembles honest conversation. I look forward to each and every book of fiction which he produces."

Philip Miller, M.D. Las Vegas, NV

"I highly recommend this very engrossing heart-warming collection of stories. Each is a joy to read. Each has a subtle message designed to teach people how to properly enjoy a satisfying life by one's self with family and others…We learn what is important in life and what is the true purpose of friendship and religion. All-in-all… They are great stories."

Rabbi Dr. Israel Drazin,
Boca Raton, FL

"VYSE AVENUE is a splendid novel that recreates the world of Jewish immigrants and their families during the 1950's. The characters are well drawn and the episodes are fascinating. I felt that I was living my life again. This book is amazing, entertaining and enjoyable. I highly recommend it."

Marilyn Stein
Montgomery Village, MD

"Always an easy read, the author's free-form style allows the reader to move from story to story effortlessly...Readers of all cultural backgrounds can understand and enjoy...a true sweet delight."
S. Violet
Huntington Station, NY

Also by Charles H. Freundlich

Vyse Avenue

Awake the Dawn

Sweet is the Light

A Crown of Beauty

A Cup of Gladness

Non-Fiction

Peretz Smolenskin: His Life and Thought

THE THIRD MOUNTAIN

By

CHARLES H. FREUNDLICH

THE THIRD MOUNTAIN

ISBN-13 978-1720479901

ISBN-10:1720479909

DEDICATED

To the Memory

OF

Shosha Hudes and Shmuel Tzvi Dworetsky

And their children

Goldie, Joseph, Ephraim, Irving

Who created families that contributed to the blossoming of Orthodox Jewish life in America

And to the Young Israel Movement

CONTENTS

PREFACE

I write these lines conscious of the deadly Covid-19 pandemic that continues to devastate the lives of thousands in America and throughout the world. I am most fortunate and grateful to God that I have been thus far spared to be able to write the closing pages of "The Third Mountain," my sixth book, since I began writing fiction on my eightieth birthday.

The chapters in this book are fictional but they are sparked by my extraordinary experiences during my career as a Rabbi and educator in many communities in America, Israel and Canada. After delivering bookish sermons and lectures for more than fifty years, I realized that a simple story that touches the heart can have a greater impact on the moral and spiritual life of my audience. Thus the simple narratives of biblical heroes: Abraham, Samson and David, still enthuse my life and writings.

Many of my themes are drawn from my youth growing up in the Bronx, New York, where I lived with my parents for nineteen years. The Bronx was a multi-cultural society comprised of Jewish, Italian, and Irish immigrants, hard-working and struggling to achieve the American Dream. That society is long gone, being replaced with new ethnic groups, also sharing the same dream.

My parents were immigrants from Eastern Europe who spoke Yiddish and experienced a vivacious legacy of Jewish culture and creativity that had all but been destroyed by the Holocaust. However, one of the great miracles of our times was the resurgence of that Jewish tradition in America beyond the dreams and hopes of my parent's generation. Another astonishing chapter in Jewish history, equally miraculous, was the rebirth of Israel, its growth of population and prosperity while emerging as a world leader in technology.

My parents with their children came to the Bronx in 1938, in the midst of the Great Depression, the rise of Nazism, and the optimism of President

Roosevelt's New Deal. Their personal triumph during these challenging years is a tribute to their hard work, total devotion to their family, religion and faith in the promise of America.

My themes in this new work deal with the clash of Jewish tradition with secular and hedonistic modernity, the social upheavals of radical individualism, loneliness, and the decline of heartfelt community, exacerbated by the prevalence of social media.

I am most indebted to my loving wife, Debby, my best friend for fifty-six years, and my most efficient editor. I am thankful to God for being blessed with a long, creative, fruitful, and happy life, which I continue to share with my family, friends, and many loyal readers.

Charles H. Freundlich   March 25, 2020
Boca Raton, Florida   29 Adar 5780

Charles H. Freundlich

THE TRIAL

Charles H. Freundlich

The Third Mountain

IT WAS a most extraordinary incident in the history of the Jewish community of Palmetto Beach, Florida; a Jewish scholar was being excommunicated for heresy. Never in the recent history of American Jewry had a respected scholar been accused of making such heinous, heretical and anti-Semitic statements publicly. Thus, a Rabbinic Court, a *Bet Din*, was convened in the city of Palmetto Beach, to bring serious charges leading to excommunication, *herem*, upon Dr. Joshua Cooper.

Most people assumed that excommunication for a scholar was an obsolete relic – an anomaly that ended with the times of Baruch Spinoza in the seventeenth century. Furthermore, numerous Jewish notables in modern Israel recently have called for the revocation of the Spinoza excommunication in lieu of the great significance of his thought in the making of the modern world.

Dr. Joshua Cooper, a young widower from New York, was long known as a trouble-maker who confused and provoked his twelfth-grade students in the local Yeshiva High School. He was a child prodigy, with a photographic memory and a free-spirited intellectual. Following his graduation from Yeshiva College and his Ph.D. from Yale University, he studied advanced Talmud in a yeshiva in Israel. An author of two books on the Bible and philosophy, he had a number of devoted readers who could fathom the profound and complex philosophical nuances of his themes. He also had a few clandestine admirers in his school faculty who considered him a positive gadfly necessary to stir up independent and original thinking in his senior Bible class.

JOSHUA COOPER'S youth and early education was an arduous and complicated journey to find a satisfying religious life. His grandparents, immigrants from Russia, were secular socialists who were active in the *Workmen's Circle, Der Arbeter Ring,* in the Bronx. They were opposed to all religion and refused to observe even the minutest ritual of Jewish tradition including attendance in synagogue on the High Holidays. They inculcated this negative attitude to Judaism to their daughter, Joshua's mother.

However, when Joshua pleaded to his mother to attend Hebrew school like all his friends, she conceded – but only for one year prior to his thirteenth birthday. Later, when Joshua cried that all his friends celebrated their Bar Mitzvah with a party and gifts, his mother conceded once again, on the condition that it would be modest and include a luncheon only for the immediate family – without relatives. From her viewpoint, entering a synagogue was deemed a betrayal of her socialist bona fides to the *Arbeter Ring.*

Young Joshua was enthralled with the biblical stories and especially the heroic sagas of Samson and King David. His Hebrew teacher, Aaron Fox, was a graduate of Yeshiva College and a doctoral candidate for Jewish studies at Columbia University. Fox was also a son of a Rabbi Zalman Fox, a charismatic Hasid, who conducted a *shtiebel* in the East Bronx.

Joshua would return home after Hebrew school excited and full of joy and exuberance from the lessons with Mr. Fox.

"Mommy, Mommy, did you know that young David slew a giant man with his slingshot?

"Mommy, Mommy, did you know that Moses split the Red Sea?

"Mommy, Mommy, are we Israelites?"

"Yes, darling, we are Israelites like Moses and David."

Mrs. Cooper was deeply concerned that she was losing her son to the ancient and backward faith that her own parents discarded when they came to America. But she could not repudiate the pleasure and exultation that she saw in her young son. He was an only child and was blossoming and happier than ever. Undoubtedly, she felt, he would outgrow his infatuation with religion.

BUT JOSHUA furthered his passion for Judaism when Mr. Fox encouraged him to attend a Jewish Day School in the Bronx. He happily attended and graduated as the valedictorian. He then furthered his religious studies at Talmudical Academy, a prestigious Jewish High School in Manhattan, and once again, graduated at the top of his class. After completing Yeshiva College, he entered Yale University where he received his Ph.D.

Joshua's mother encouraged him to pursue a career in academia and his resume was submitted to both Harvard and Columbia which had significant Jewish studies programs. During this time, he authored a number of scholarly papers on the Bible which were published in the New England Bible Quarterly. His studies were radical, created a commotion in academic circles and were harshly condemned. Cooper had denied the widely-accepted belief by most bible scholars that Moses was a fictitious character and that the Pentateuch was written hundreds of years after the classical prophetic age. Cooper argued, in his well-documented paper, that this academic time-honored thesis was dubious and needed to be reconsidered.

He was decried by one scholar as reactionary and medieval. How dare this novice challenge well-accepted scholarly theories which were more than a hundred years old? His papers were ridiculed in the following editions of the Bible Quarterly. Six months after submitting his resume to Harvard, he received a brief response. His application for an appointment to teach was rejected. The faculty did not approve of his unscholarly and reactionary views.

Mrs. Cooper was greatly disappointed and distraught. But Joshua was not surprised. "I think my rejection by Harvard was warranted, Mom," he said. "After all, academicians look upon the Bible as ancient literature to be studied scientifically and objectively. I, however, consider the Bible holy and its words inspired by God. Academicians are supposed to seek the truth wherever it may lead. I also seek the truth, but most important, the Bible is Torah, guidance for a Jew to live in God's way. No, Mom, I think I would be more suited to teach in an Orthodox Hebrew High School where I can inspire my students to live a spiritual life."

JOSHUA COOPER'S teaching career in Jewish high schools was personally very gratifying and he continued to write numerous scholarly papers on the Bible in addition to book-reviews, short articles and portraits of Jewish life. He was highly successful wherever he taught, including schools in New York and Boston, for more than eight years.

He married Susan Rosen, a Hebrew teacher, whom he met while vacationing in the Evergreen Hotel. But his joyous marriage turned to harsh tragedy when Susan died in labor during her first pregnancy. Joshua was without comfort after Susan's death. He felt he needed a change in venue and came to Palmetto Beach in Florida to teach Bible in its prestigious Yeshiva High School.

But his sorrow after losing Susan was not diminished and he delved into writing a series of short stories. He found in Palmetto Beach a most desirable community with its excellent beaches, convivial weather, well-organized Jewish Community Center and numerous vibrant synagogues filled with youthful and affluent families. The number of kosher restaurants was an added feature. Was this not a haven for Joshua Cooper, a widower, desiring to build a new life?

WHILE TEACHING at the Yeshiva High School, he once declared, "Just because the students of this high school are Orthodox, it does not mean that they are unable to think boldly, independently and outside the box." The principal of the high school, who surreptitiously was also a devotee of Dr. Cooper, was placed in a most precarious position. His contract was up the following year and his Board of Directors was outraged by his overlooking the most egregious calumnies Cooper made to his graduating students regarding the Holocaust, the Daily Talmud Study Program, *Daf Yomi*, and the sanctity of Israel.

After enduring severe parental pressure, the principal acquiesced to the dismissal of Dr. Cooper. That was not sufficient for the Board of Directors. They argued that Dr. Cooper may accept a post in another Yeshiva High School and continue to corrupt other young Jewish minds with his unOrthodox teachings. Cooper's credentials and reputation must be so demolished, they insisted, so that he would never be accepted as a teacher in any Jewish school. Nothing less than excommunication, *herem,* from the Jewish community by a renowned Orthodox Rabbinic Court, *Bet Din,* must be imposed upon him to neutralize his heretical doctrines forever.

AND WHAT were these so-called un-Orthodox, heretical, and dangerous ideas asserted by Dr. Cooper that so enraged the parents of his twelfth grade?

The first was his assertion that anti-Semitism was not the major cause of the Holocaust but a consequence of the social condition of the Jews themselves. In addition, he was opposed to the centrality of Holocaust memory and the ideology of victimhood in contemporary Jewish life.

These deeply offensive ideas expressed to his class the day before the school's annual *Yom*

Hashoah program, elicited boisterous and rowdy responses from the parents and numerous phone calls to the principal demanding that Cooper be dismissed immediately. "Incredible," one parent shouted, "a Holocaust-denier in our own school!" Other parents were children of Holocaust survivors and felt painfully offended.

AFTER investigation, it was discovered that this was not the only extremely radical idea that Cooper expressed to his students. As the parents gathered in protestation in the principal's office it was learned that Cooper ridiculed the massive gatherings in sports stadiums to celebrate the seven-year completion of Talmud study known as the *Daf Yomi* Program. Indeed, he argued that the celebrated Talmud educational program was ill-conceived and a waste of time! "How outrageous," one parent lamented. "*Daf Yomi* is the most successful manifestation of universal Torah commitment. It is testimony of Orthodox Judaism's vitality and the glorious triumph over the assimilationist, and deteriorating liberal branches of Judaism that have almost exterminated American Judaism!" A so-called colleague of Cooper proclaimed, "This degrading of Talmud study, the most important *mitzvah,* was a desecration of the name of God, a horrific *Chillul Hashem.*"

It was also revealed that Cooper had commented to a fellow teacher, "If you put a tent over Tel Aviv it would be the biggest whore-house in the Middle East." This provoked Selma Roth, President of Hadassah, who added her name and organization to the cause of excommunicating Cooper.

RABBI LEIBEL GROSS, well respected for his scholarship and piety, was approached by Chaim Lieber, President of the Board of Directors of the Yeshiva High School for his assistance. Would he serve as the head of the Bet Din?

Rabbi Gross's answer was swift and shocking. "I have been recently approached by Dr. Cooper, who revealed the plans for excommunicating him. I have known Dr. Cooper for only one year since his coming to Palmetto Beach and have had lengthy and vigorous discussions with him in my synagogue. I respect him, though I do not agree with him in many matters. In fact, he made some serious and outrageous accusations against the entire Chabad moment."

"I find it hard to criticize the Chabad movement with its global outreach of more than four-thousand *sheluchim*, emissaries," Lieber responded.

"He did more than just criticize, Mr. Lieber. He actually decried the entire movement as a fraud and a waste of time. First, he noted that the movement lacks transparency both in its financial and religious accomplishments. Most individual branches do not require dues. Nor are there any treasurers to report detailed finances. What organization is so secretive as to be above probity?

"Secondly," Cooper argued, "there are no Boards of Directors giving a voice to the people who contribute unaccountable donations to sustain the numerous branches. And thirdly, and most important, there is no proof that the full-time efforts of four thousand emissaries actually transform many Jews into a religious lifestyle.

"Perhaps they will persuade a Jew off the street to put on *tefillin* once, or eat Hanukkah latkes for free in outdoor candle lighting. But hardly any authentic Orthodox Jews attend the Chabad shuls. Those attracted to Chabad shuls are mostly the marginal - the misfits, former druggies, backpackers in Nepal and those who want a low-cost Hebrew and Bar Mitzvah program with no obligation to pay annual dues. One would think that the serious and committed four thousand *sheluchim* would accomplish more for Judaism. But lacking authoritative facts, it is estimated that only a few hundred Jews each year are transformed to lead an authentic Orthodox way of life."

I REPLIED to Cooper, "Every Jewish soul is important to our mission to ignite sparks of *Yiddishkeit*. Better some living sparks for the soul to ignite than have complete darkness."

BUT Cooper argued, "Instead of training an army of emissaries for a few minor ritual improvements, Chabad should provide a modern higher education to these same *sheluchim* to become doctors, lawyers, scientists, and journalists to help the poor, defend the powerless, and promote justice for the downtrodden, like our ancient prophets.

"How do you know that among these four thousand *sheluchim,* denied a modern education and raised in isolated communities, there is not a budding: Jonas Salk, Selma Waksman, Rene Cassin, Saul Bellow, Milton Friedman or a Louis Brandeis, being crushed? Is it not a shame that among the two hundred Jewish Nobel Prize winners who advanced modern civilization and progress, virtually all were non-Orthodox? What would have happened if these two hundred Jews, the vanguard of modern science, literature, and medicine, were converted to the cloistered and backward education and lifestyle of Chabad Orthodoxy? Perhaps millions of people would have died or suffered needlessly without their achievements!"

I RESPONDED, "My dear Dr. Cooper, if we are so backward, how can you explain our incredible success and acceptance throughout the modern world? Even the Reform leaders admit that we are the largest and most effective Jewish religious movement in the world."

Dr. COOPER responded in the vilest way: "My dear Rabbi, I admit that your movement is highly successful in expanding and building numerous branches but not in selling its product – Orthodox Judaism. Your *sheluchim* are master salesmen and employ the oldest gimmick for con-artists. First, they offer free personal services, or a free Shabbos meal, or *latkes,* which motivate people to feel guilty that they owe something. Then they solicit them for money in the name of authentic religion and hastening the Messiah. What happens to this guilt money? Indeed, the beards and black hats of the *sheluchim* are only a façade to represent the so-called genuine Orthodox Jewish religion and serve as a trigger to naïve Jews to offer generous funds to build more branches that serve no one - but provide a job for most of the *sheluchim* who lack a basic modern education or a profession."

RABBI GROSS continued, "As you can see, Mr. Lieber, Dr. Cooper is a typical American youth infected with the disease of narcissism, radical individualism and self-fulfillment. He could hardly appreciate the fact that our *sheluchim* are imbued with a devout faith in the leadership of our Rebbe, Hasidism and a 100% commitment to living a total Torah lifestyle to hasten the coming of the Messiah. Their passion, *mesiras nefesh*, for self-sacrificing duty to the cause of Torah, has enabled them to succeed in the four corners of the earth and command the respect of Jews both secular and religious. Fortunately, their loyalty to Yiddishkeit, not a personal career, has made them the most effective movement for Jewish revival.

"In spite of his venomous attack on my own faith, Dr. Cooper has asked me to serve as his attorney if there is to be a formal trial with a Bet Din. Needless to say, I think the idea of excommunicating Cooper will make him a heroic martyr. Numerous liberal outsiders will support him in the cause of freedom of speech and expression. I think it is more than adequate that Dr. Cooper has been dismissed from his post. You are stirring up a hornet's nest that will divide the Jewish community and make a mockery of Modern Orthodox Judaism. Go home, Mr. Lieber, and have a restful sleep. You will have better judgment in the morning."

CHAIM LIEBER was not to be frustrated in his mission to have Dr. Cooper excommunicated by an authorized Orthodox Bet Din. He next turned to the distinguished Rabbi of the Palmetto Beach Synagogue, Israel Broder. Under the dynamic leadership of Rabbi Broder, The Palmetto Beach Synagogue known as PBS had become the most prestigious Orthodox Synagogue in the South Eastern region of the United States. Its renowned adult educational program was reported in noted Orthodox journals. It engaged many prestigious scholars from New York and Israel to serve as *Scholars in Residence* and featured numerous classes in Bible, Jewish history and Halacha that attracted hundreds each week.

Its more than seven hundred members included many retired Rabbis and Cantors in addition to many medical professionals, lawyers and financiers. An Assistant Rabbi served the more than one thousand youth and teenagers for Shabbat and

Sunday activities, and also aggressive outreach program for the non-Orthodox. Highlighting its educational roster of Torah studies was its vaunted *Daf Yomi*, daily Talmud study classes, held both in the morning and evening.

DR.COOPER was enthusiastic to worship and participate in this outstanding synagogue when he arrived in Palmetto Beach a year earlier, to teach Bible in the Yeshiva High School. He introduced himself to Rabbi Broder in the vestibule following Sabbath services but the latter was surrounded by many members eager to share a brief moment. Cooper was somewhat disappointed when the Rabbi said, "I'd love to spend some time with you, Dr. Cooper, and share some ideas. Perhaps you can call me at my office for an appointment."

Cooper was delighted when he met a familiar face from the Bronx, Attorney Henry Bloom.
"Great to see you again, Henry. How long have you been living in Palmetto Beach?"
"Three years, since my retirement. You came to the right place, Josh. Our synagogue is the best in the country."

"I'm honored to be here in the *best synagogue* in the country. I hope they'll permit me to daven here."

"I didn't mean to be snobbish, Josh. But this is really a great shul with a lot of high-class members."

"You mean this is an exclusive elitist shul?"

"I mean that there are many successful doctors and lawyers and investment executives, with lots of money."

"Thanks for telling me how lucky and privileged I am - a plain high school teacher, in the company of such exclusive people."

"We must get together, Josh. I'll give you a call."

AFTER attending the Palmetto Beach Synagogue on Sabbath for six months, Cooper was approached by a short, stocky man. "Shalom, I'm Joseph Heller, the *Chief Gabbai*. I noticed that you are new here. I hope you will join and become a member of our wonderful synagogue."

"I will certainly consider it, Mr. Heller. By the way, my name is Dr. Joshua Cooper. It's nice to meet you, Mr. Heller."

Dr. Cooper also attended the daily 7:00 A.M minyan during the same period of time. He introduced himself to the *Minyan Gabbai*, Carl

Gordon. This was one of five daily minyanim each morning.

One evening during his exercises at the local Jewish Community Center, Cooper fell and injured his neck. After a few treatments of physical therapy he returned to the minyan two weeks later.

The *Gabbai* greeted him, "I noticed you were absent for a while. Were you ill? I would have called you but I didn't know your name."

"My name is Dr. Joshua Cooper."

When the services were over, Cooper reflected: I worshipped here for six months almost every day and the Gabbai didn't even know my name! I don't think I belong here.

A WEEK later, Dr. Coper received a phone call from the secretary of Rabbi Israel Broder. "Hello, Dr. Cooper, I am calling on behalf of the Rabbi. We know that you are new here and we would like to formally welcome you. Next week, we are having a special Kiddush welcoming the new members and we hope you will be able to attend. The Rabbi would like to meet you personally."

Cooper replied, "I will be glad to attend though I have not yet decided to become a member. By the way, if the Rabbi would like to meet me personally, I attend Shabbat services regularly, or he can contact me personally by phone during the week after 6:00 P.M. Thank you for the invitation."

Cooper attended the Kiddush for new members and he was approached by a tall man with a wisp of grey hair. "Shalom and Gut Shabbos, welcome to *PBS* –as we refer to our synagogue. I'm Dr. Hershel Kagan, President, and am delighted that you have chosen to worship here. By the way my Dental Office is on Atlantic Avenue and we give our PBS members a 10% discount. My sources tell me that you teach Bible at the Yeshiva High School and you have written numerous books."

"I'm pleased to meet you," Cooper returned. "I have just published my fourth volume of Jewish stories, all filled with Jewish values and ideals. I would be delighted to provide a free lecture for the congregation about my latest book."

"Thank you, but I don't handle these matters."

"No? Who does?"

"Well, the Rabbi takes care of the adult education program and the planning for the numerous visiting lecturers."

"I understand. Anyway I have a copy with me in my *tallis* bag and you can have this copy."

"Thank you, very much."

"By the way, Dr. Kagan, I read the illustrious PBS weekly bulletin and note its wonderful articles by the Rabbi and the details of the many exciting forthcoming services and educational programs. But I have not seen any articles or reports by you, the President, or any other of the officers or your Board of Directors."

"Oh, the Bulletin is the Rabbi's project. He is very talented and diligent and does most of the articles and selection of visiting Rabbis and scholars."

"You must have an easy job as President of such a large and active congregation where the Rabbi seems to do everything."

"Yes, the Rabbi is very talented, hardworking and dedicated to the congregation. We are so fortunate to have such an outstanding scholar for our spiritual leader."

"May I offer a suggestion, Dr. Kagan? As President, you make the announcements following services. Would it not be a good idea to personally thank those members who lead the services – the Torah Reader, the *ba'al shacharis* and *ba'al mussaf*? I know that in many synagogues this practice is done. People like to hear their names and to be recognized for their service publicly, and they are disheartened when their contributions are ignored."

"I shall consult the Rabbi about this suggestion. Thank you."

THE FOLLOWING week, Cooper brought his latest book to the Rabbi's office and handed it to the secretary. He inscribed this note on the first page:

For Rabbi Israel Broder,

Yasher Koach, May you continue to serve your congregation with inspiring lectures and sermons. I hope you will find my book interesting and would appreciate any suggestions or criticism.

Sincerely, Joshua Cooper

Cooper waited a week and did not receive a thank-you letter or phone call from the Rabbi. He phoned the office and inquired from the secretary if the Rabbi had received his book. "Yes, Dr. Cooper. I handed the envelope with your book personally to the Rabbi. You know the Rabbi is very busy. In fact he is in Washington attending a special reception for clergy in the White House. He'll be back Friday morning."

THE LETTER was very brief: Dear Dr. Cooper: Please be advised that the Bet Din of Palmetto Beach has requested your presence at a hearing on June 18 at 10:00 A.M. in Beth Israel Congregation regarding your dismissal from the Yeshiva High School.

Sincerely, Rabbi Isaac Silver, Av Bet Din.

Cooper had expected this letter and appeared promptly at 10:00 A.M.

Rabbi Silver was accompanied by two other well-known Rabbis from the County. They sat at a large desk in the Board Room of Beth Israel Congregation and Dr. Cooper was asked to remain standing during the hearing.

Rabbi Silver began. "The purpose of this hearing, Dr. Cooper, is to consider two urgent matters regarding your standing in the Jewish Community of Palmetto Beach and also your dismissal from the Yeshiva High School.

"First, let me say, with total surprise, that Rabbi Leibel Gross, a distinguished colleague and *Talmid Chacham*, and head of the local Chabad, has informed us in writing that he opposes any condemnation of you as a devout and observant Orthodox Jew. While he disagrees with many of your ideas, he feels your intent is *l'Shem Shamayim*, motivated by authentic Jewish values and ideals. He urges us to dismiss any charges of *herem*, excommunication, and also recommends that you be allowed to return to your teaching post at the Yeshiva High School. We were all surprised by Rabbi Gross's defense and we will consider it seriously.

"We also have a written petition from six of your fellow teachers at the Yeshiva High School approving of your character and viewpoints and asking that you be returned to your post.

"Most important, Dr. Cooper, is this letter from Mr. Chaim Lieber, President of the Board of Directors of the Yeshiva High School, who argues most strongly, that you are very dangerous to young students and should be excommunicated lest you find employment in another Jewish school where you may continue your venemous and heretical un-Orthodox views.

"We are convened as a Bet Din on behalf of these petitions because of the uproar that has divided and weakened this peaceful and harmonious Jewish community. Unfortunately, Rabbi Broder is in Israel and cannot participate. Do you understand these charges, Dr. Cooper?"

"I understand perfectly and if given a chance I plan to defend myself against these bigoted and scurrilous charges."

"LET us proceed," Rabbi Silver announced.

"First, there is the serious accusation that you vilified Eretz Yisrael, our holy land, by claiming that Tel Aviv was the biggest *whore-house* in the Middle

East. Is that true? This is tantamount to *dibas ha-aretz,* the slandering of Israel by the ten spies."

"What I asserted, Rabbi Silver, was that if you placed a tent over Tel Aviv it would be the largest whore-house in the Middle East."

"Are you not guilty of defaming Eretz Yisrael, by this malicious insult to your students? Do you not realize that the Yeshiva High School is deeply committed to the cause of Zionism and encourages Aliyah? You have flagrantly abused your mission to inspire the love of Israel in the hearts and souls of our students! How do you plead?"

"I am both guilty and not guilty."

"Please explain your contradictory response."

"I can explain my so-called offensive statement with this true but simple story, if you allow the time."

"You may proceed, Dr. Cooper. We are in no rush to deal with this serious accusation."

"Please bear with me, Rabbi, as I relate this true story about this controversial statement. A number of years ago, one of my best friends, Allen Green, was on the ship, S.S. Jerusalem, to Israel for a year's study in a yeshiva. Allen was an ardent Zionist and had served as a *madrich,* leader, for one of the Zionist chapters in the Bronx. Anyway, Allen, a zealous Zionist, was having a conversation with an older Israeli returning to his home in Tel Aviv. This older Israeli was trying to orient the idealistic Allen about life in Israel and made this shocking statement, 'If you put tent over Tel Aviv it would be the largest whore-house in the Middle East.'

"Needless to say, Allen was deeply astounded and offended. Allen spent numerous weekends in Tel Aviv and was thrilled with its energy which captured the spirit of Israel reborn. Allen suppressed the false and odious statement about Tel Aviv and it remained buried deep in his mind."

"Is that the end of the story, Dr. Cooper?"

"Not quite, Rabbi. Let me continue. Allen continued to make trips to Israel for the next twenty years and further increased his love and admiration for both Jerusalem and Tel Aviv. He lamented that his personal state of affairs did not permit his going on Aliyah with his family. Now here is the crux of the story.

"In the next twenty years the world, especially the western democracies and America, were transformed radically in regards to fundamental social mores about family, feminism and sex. Allen had pursued a career as a Rabbi and was deeply loyal to traditional Torah ideals regarding family values.

"One day, while Allen had a pulpit in Newark, New Jersey, a cousin of his was coming to America with his Newark-born bride to get married. He asked to spend the night in Allen's home for the evening with his bride before the wedding not far from Newark. Naturally, Allen and his wife were delighted. They asked his cousin and bride to spend the evening in separate bedrooms, much to their surprise. Allen explained that they were Orthodox and this was their tradition.

"The following summer, Allen made one of his numerous trips to Tel Aviv to visit his relatives. While there, Nurit, his cousin's mother, grinned in derision, and declared, 'Allen dear, you have become the laughing stock of Tel Aviv, by asking my son and his bride-to be to sleep in separate rooms. Don't you know that today all young people sleep together before marriage?'

"Allen responded, "That may be true for secular Israelis but it is not true for religious girls and boys. Sexual relations before or outside of marriage is considered *zenut,* whoring!'

"Nurit was enraged, 'How dare you call it *zenut!* Times have changed! All boys and girls in Tel Aviv have sex before marriage!'

"Some things don't change," Allen responded.

"At that moment, Allen recalled the shocking comment of his fellow passenger, made twenty years earlier. Of course, Tel Aviv was and is a modern western city in the midst of an Islamic world with a strict traditional sexual code forbidding open and liberal sex. From the perspective of the Islamic culture, Tel Aviv was then, and is, the biggest whore-house in the Middle East, no different than other non-Islamic Western cities like Paris, New York and London.

"Rabbi, what I said was true. I love Israel with all my heart and I love Tel Aviv. But, the fact is – Tel Aviv is recognized throughout the world as the most attractive and welcoming city for Gays and Lesbians. I still believe the Biblical rule that these forms of sex are a *toevah*, an abomination. My assertion about Tel Aviv is true from a Torah perspective. I might add that Western cities like Miami and Palmetto Beach are just as depraved as Tel Aviv. They are also *whore-houses...That,* is my defense."

RABBI SILVER paused a minute to reflect. Then, in a soft tone, said that he would ask Rabbi Baruch Karlin of the Beth Israel Congregation to offer a response on behalf of the Bet Din.

"I FIRST wish to commend you, Dr. Cooper, for your courage to speak out when it is no longer *politically correct* to be critical or dismissive about liberal sex values, Gays and Lesbians. We of the Torah community are a small minority in liberal American society, and even a minority among the liberal Jewish community, and we have to be circumspect what we say publicly. I speak for my colleagues, when I say that we were disheartened and disgusted to learn about the recent Gay Pride Parade in Jerusalem, our holy city.

"Nevertheless, there are some egregious errors in your defense. First, you must acknowledge that Tel Aviv was the city from whence David Ben-Gurion declared the birth of Israel in 1948. It was then the capitol and remains the heart of Israel's population and culture. It is the vanguard of the advances in science and technology and economic development of Israel. Most significant of all, the youth – boys and girls - are the main source of Israel's Defense forces.

"The youth of Tel Aviv are the ones who will spill their blood and fight the wars to defend Israel – so that those in the yeshivas in Bnai Brak and Jerusalem can study Torah full-time. Make no mistake, Tel Aviv *is modern Israel*. While I cannot condone the sexual mores of the citizens of Tel

Aviv, which violate the Torah, I must take cognizance of the magnificent contributions they have made to all of Israel and the Jews throughout the world.

"And that, my dear Dr. Cooper, is where your harsh criticism of Tel Aviv fell short and, I might add, was misleading and erroneous. You should have emphasized the great virtues and creative contributions about Tel Aviv before you expressed the negative criticism. Your statement lacked balance and perspective. It failed to live up to the principle of *words of scholars are offered with pleasantness* – not insensitivity.

"You might have said that Tel Aviv was flawed and deficient from the perspective of traditional Orthodox sexual mores, like all modern cities, but *not worse. Deficient* is a more appropriate word than *whore-house.*

"I understand that you are highly original and outspoken in your religious ideals. Many of the great ideas of our people including Zionism, Hasidism, were once thought to be radical views of crazy people and condemned. I admire your audacity and courage to speak your mind and I do not think you are insane. Indeed, Ignaz Semmelweis, the pioneer who advocated the washing of hands for nurses and doctors before touching their patients in the 1840's, was deemed insane, and thrown into an asylum where he shortly died.

"I wish you well and hope that you will continue to express your unpopular views – but with a little more balance. I do not find you guilty of *dibas ha-aretz*, slandering the land of Israel. That is my judgement."

RABBI SILVER continued, "I have asked Rabbi Dr. Benjamin Dubnov of the Palmetto Jewish Center to discuss your unusual assertion about the Holocaust and anti-Semitism. Rabbi Dr. Dubnov has a Ph.D. in Jewish history from Brandeis University and is especially endowed with the knowledge to judge your unusual views."

"I do not think them unusual since I can support them with numerous historical facts."

"I believe you can, Dr. Cooper," Rabbi Dubnov began. "But I would like to make clear a number of undeniable facts. First, the number of Holocaust survivors is dwindling rapidly and many are over ninety years of age and some are becoming senile. Secondly, the Holocaust-denial movement is increasing, particularly in Poland and Lithuania where it has become illegal to assert the complicity of their populations with the Nazis.

"These countries with a long history of anti-Semitism were the most venomous during the Holocaust. In fact, the last Pope, on behalf of the Catholic Church, issued a statement on the Shoah recognizing and apologizing for its long history of anti-Semitism. It is therefore most alarming to hear that the historic authenticity of the greatest crime against the Jews in human history is being denied and its memory challenged by an Orthodox educator with excellent academic credentials and Israeli *semicha!* What have you to say to justify your assertion that historic anti-Semitism was not the root cause of the Holocaust?

"I UNDERSTAND your deep distress, Rabbi Dubnov, and I would like to clarify my belief that the Holocaust was unique and not the result of historic anti-Semitism in Germany, Lithuania or Poland," Cooper argued.

Rabbi Dubnov continued, "I assume that you have heard of the execution of thousands of Lithuanian Jews in Ponar by the native militias - not the Nazis – and similar atrocities on Jews in a few Polish towns like Jedwadne. And precisely in countries with a long history of anti-Semitism, the tragedy of the Holocaust was most severe."

Cooper responded, "I agree with these facts, Rabbi. But let me clarify my view that the Holocaust was not a result of historic anti-Semitism but of more egregious political, social and economic conditions.

"Let me begin by noting that no country with a long history of anti-Semitism: France, England, United States and Germany, and the Catholic Church has ever devised a similar genocidal ideology before Hitler. During the 1930's anti-Semitism was more rampant in the United States than any European country - greater than Germany, greater than Stalin's Russia. In fact, during the most horrendous pogroms of Tsarist Russia in the 1880's, there was no genocidal plan similar to the Nazis.

"The most extreme policy emanating from the Tsarist regime was the solution of Pobyedonostev, advisor to Alexander III: one third of the Jews was to emigrate, one third was to be converted, and one third was to die of hunger. Not even in the 12th century, the zenith of the power of the Catholic Church, was there a plan to murder all the Jews. Not even in Queen Isabella's Spain at the height of its power, was there any genocidal plan against the Jews - only expulsion.

"When did the Holocaust begin? The date will reveal the true origins of the Holocaust. According to Dr. Yehuda Bauer, the dean of Holocaust studies, and Director of Yad Vashem, the Holocaust began in June 1942, when Hitler broke his treaty with the Soviet Union, and invaded its occupied Polish region. In Hitler's paranoiac mind, the myth of the international Jewish communist was conflated with the Soviet Union, the home of International Communism. While most Jews were not communists, numerous leading high profile communists were Jews: Rosa Luxemburg, Kurt Eisner, Bela Kun, and Leon Trotsky. The Soviet Union was the greatest obstacle to Hitler's imagined expansion, *lebensraum*, and was deemed necessary to be destroyed.

"At the same time, Hitler conflated Communism with Judaism and initiated the Holocaust. It was the false myth of International Jewish Communism that threatened Hitler's paranoiac and psychopathic mind – not historic, religious, political or social anti-Semitism. I might add, that one of the great Jewish historians of the Holocaust asserted that the sick mind of Hitler, not the historic German social anti-Semitism, was the genesis of the Holocaust."

RABBI DUBNOV replied, "An interesting theory, Dr. Cooper, but how do you explain the violent murders of Jews in The Tree of Life Synagogue in Pittsburgh, Monsey and in the Kosher Market in Jersey City? Were these ruthless murders not a consequence of anti-Semitism?"

Dr. Cooper replied, "These incidents were, no doubt, products of anti-Semitism, as was the lynching of Leo Frank in 1912. However, virtually all attacks on Jews and Blacks and similar attacks on public school children in Parkland, Florida, or Sandy Hook, Connecticut, were performed by disturbed teenagers and unhinged young whites from dysfunctional homes.

"Consider the statistics: There are 4,000 synagogues in the United States, which have at least one service per week, constituting 208,000 possibilities for terror annually. Over the last one hundred years, there were over 20,800,000 opportunities to attack Jews on the Sabbath in synagogues. Can you name more than three anti-Semitic acts while Jews were in synagogues?

"However, what is most significant is that no overtly anti-Semitic candidate can be elected, in any federal, state or municipal election in the United Sates today. Only people of political power and social standing like the paranoiac Hitler may constitute a serious threat to Jews, not sick, dysfunctional individuals on the margins of society.

"My conclusion: Anti-Semitism is not a serious threat to American Jews today. However, if you conflate anti-Semitism and the Holocaust with its theme of victimization, it becomes an overstated, alarming and frightening danger.

"Only a paranoic, absolute *fuhrer*, dictator, who was above the law, with a compliant population, could have implemented the Holocaust – a unique historical tragedy in Jewish and German history."

RABBI SILVER suggested, "I think we have accomplished much this morning as a Bet Din. I suggest that we have a recess for lunch and continue our deliberations at 2:00 P.M. Agreed?

The three Rabbis entered the private office of Rabbi Karlin for lunch and also to review their previous deliberation.

"I believe we have achieved much of our goals regarding Dr. Cooper," Rabbi Silver declared. "What is your assessment, Rabbi Karlin? Has Cooper expressed any unOrthodox, heretical or dangerous ideas to his students? Are we engaged in a bizarre endeavor which will render the Modern Orthodox community both ridiculous and outdated?"

Rabbi Karlin responded, "Dr. Cooper is an iconoclast, like Abraham our Patriarch. Our senior students do not need to be confused, stirred up or shocked, regarding their Zionist aspirations and ideals. Their minds are most impressionable and they may become disillusioned by the radical and acerbic ideas of Cooper. However, the idea of *herem*, excommunication, which must be based on malicious intent, is absent from Cooper's statements. I suspect that you are right. We have been tricked into this anachronistic procedure by a fanatical Chaim Lieber, President of the Board of the High School Yeshiva.

"Now, let's hear what he has to say about the study of Torah and the Daf Yomi. I believe that you, Rabbi Silver, as Av Bet Din and a teacher of Daf Yomi in your synagogue, ought to be evaluating his very bizarre and hostile ideas."

THE BET DIN gathered in the main auditorium and was surprised to see a number of reporters from the Jewish Community Weekly, the Daily Sun Sentinel and the Miami Herald, in addition to a crowd of more than two hundred people.

Rabbi Karlin explained, to his colleagues, "The news of the Bet Din gathering for an excommunication deliberation reached the ears of many religious leaders outside our community. In addition, a number of social justice warriors came uninvited to our synagogue to protest our activities and support Cooper as a martyr for free speech.

"Apparently, the news of an excommunication in our age was deemed sensational and was of interest not only to our Orthodox community but to the entire Jewish community. It was impossible to continue this rabbinical proceeding behind closed doors. I had to permit their entrance. Indeed, there are rumors that we seek to excommunicate the entire non-Orthodox Jewish community and become totally segregated, like the German Jewish community of Frankfurt of Rabbi Samson Raphael Hirsch in the previous century!"

Rabbi Dubnov added, "Apparently we have been duped into assuaging the opinion of our most extreme elements, like we always do. We have always been looking over our right shoulder hoping not to arouse the condemnation of the *Yeshivish* faction from Brooklyn and Lakewood."

Rabbi Silver was alarmed, "I'm not fearful of what our right-wing Orthodox extremists will say; I am fearful of what our own Modern Orthodox congregants will say. Have we not betrayed our commitment to embrace both modernity, and American values to our Torah way of life? Modernity means *openness* to new ideas, not condemning those ideas with which we feel uncomfortable.

"Our extremists, like Chaim Lieber and his cohort, will call our acceptance of modernity a *Chilul Hashem*. But our modern educated Orthodox members will note a deep sense of our weakness and failure to stand up for our values and capitulation to the right-wing. My friends, we will conclude this Bet Din in about an hour and inform the crowd and the reporters that we will answer their questions after 3:00 P.M. Let us now hear from Dr. Cooper and his extreme and negative views of our Daf Yomi movement."

DR. COOPER began: "The reason I criticized the worth of the Daf Yomi program is simple – it does not teach. It glosses over difficult, arcane and complex texts as if they emanated from a simpleton – not from brilliant Rabbis.

"Let me draw my arguments from my own years of Talmud study in a yeshiva. My first years of Talmud study were spent in the Talmudical Academy of Manhattan where the Jewish studies program was from 9:00 A.M through 1:00 P.M., five days a week. The first two hours were set aside for our preparation for the two-hour lectures delivered by our Rebbi. At the end of the week, having devoted twenty hours of devoted study, we usually completed one *blatt*, two sides of a page. As a matter of fact, at the end of the year we completed abut forty blatt.

"This same level of progress continued in my college years at Yeshiva College where the hours were from 9:00 A.M. through 3:00 P.M. and the amount covered was little more than forty blatt. At a Brooklyn Mesivta, the hours were from 9:00 A.M. through 5:00 P.M., and we covered hardly more text.

"I was privileged to hear the lectures from some of the great scholars of our age. Thus, it was normal to complete about one blatt of Talmud in twenty to thirty-five hours per week.

"The Daf Yomi plan requires the completion of a blatt in one hour – one twentieth of the time! Now, unless all the yeshivas I attended were dysfunctional and wasteful, why were they allotting twenty times as much as the noted Daf Yomi program?

"The fact is, the Talmud is not written or organized like a modern book – the subject matter is legalistic, non-thematic and the discussions and dialectics are based on a Babylonian logic often foreign to western logic, and the conclusions are often indecisive, *teiku,* confusing and perplexing. But the reason twenty hours are devoted to a blatt is because the Talmud is the Oral Torah, the source of our spiritual life and the extensive effort is a mitzvah.

"Fortunately, the writing of later codes like the Mishneh Torah and the Shulchan Aruch, simplified the complex and difficult legalistic, *halachic,* body of the Oral Torah for the common Jew by concentrating on one legal theme at a time for each chapter. Today, we live by these later codes of law and not directly by the Chumash or Babylonian Talmud. However, the Babylonian Talmud is studied as the root and basis of all later codes including the Rabbinic Responsa of today.

"It took the genius of Maimonides to reorganize and translate the Talmud into Hebrew for the common man as a rational and practical guide for a Torah life. Serious and effective Talmud study was reserved only for those who could devote numerous hours each day and not as a superficial endeavor

"The Daf Yomi undervalues the study of Talmud which deserves great effort and devotion. It is also impractical for the huge amount of complex ideas that are quickly forgotten – in one ear and out the other. Since much of the Talmudic dialectics and laws are theoretical but not *k'halacha,* not practiced, they are simply forgotten. You know the educational principle; *if you don't use it you lose it.*

"I might add an interesting note about the gravity of Talmud study. When I was a student at the Brooklyn Mesivta, for two years, a local printer was producing inexpensive photo-offset editions of the complete Babylonian Talmud. One was a small 5X8 four-volume, complete set of the Talmud for $9.95. My Rebbi was furious! How dare they produce a complete Shas, normally twenty volumes and bound beautifully in leather - the pride of a scholar's library - so cheaply! The price cheapens the Talmud! I own this small set today, but have purchased a larger, normal size, twenty-volume edition, for my library."

"ARE YOU suggesting that Talmud study is impractical or unimportant? Rabbi Silver asked.

Dr. Cooper replied, "No, I am suggesting that it is *so important* that we study as much as we can absorb and remember, in a limited amount of time. I study Talmud every day from Torah Tapes designed for the Daf Yomi program, one blatt on one-hour tapes. However, I devote about one week for the blatt. I know by experience, that our maximum attention span for sermons or serious lectures is about eighteen minutes. I divide my daily Torah studies into three subjects – Tanach - Bible, Halacha

- Rambam or Shulchan Aruch - and Talmud from the Daf Yomi tapes. This program works for me and I have been a professional educator for thirty years."

RABBI SILVER replied, "I cannot argue about what works for you and I encourage you to study Talmud and Torah in your way. But the Daf Yomi is a universal program for all Jews and it works well judging by the enormous gatherings on the seven year completion *Siyum* in titanic sports stadiums. Daf Yomi works for the Jewish people and encourages even simple, unsophisticated Jews to be part of a great endeavor. In a war - and we Orthodox Jews are fighting a great war - against assimilation into a society that is hostile to religion, atheistic, hedonistic, and ego-centered. Even simple Jews, foot soldiers, who partake of Daf Yomi will be inspired, and uplifted knowing that they part of God's army and are connected to the generals, the great Talmudic scholars.

"My dear Dr. Cooper, I respect your sincere and heartfelt views even though I believe they are erroneous. You are not guilty of any breach of Torah law and I herewith conclude the deliberations of this Bet Din.

"And now, we will consider any questions or comments from the reporters or audience."

\

THE REPORT

Charles H. Freundlich

The Third Mountain

ON THE AFTERNOON OF JULY 8, a group of five Conservative Rabbis, all members of The Rabbinical Assembly, gathered at the Monticello Hotel to review a most controversial recent report about the state of Conservative Judaism. Authored by Professor Jack Wertheimer, a distinguished member of the faculty of their Seminary, the Report generated a furor throughout their movement. Rabbi Milton Golden, the Chairperson, of this special committee, was asked to review the Report and offer criticism and recommendations to the general assembly of the Rabbis at their forthcoming annual convention.

Milton opened, "First order of business: I thank you all for coming to this first of three meetings in this luxurious resort in the scenic Catskills. And second, I ordered Room Service to bring us a delicious dinner so we can have our meeting uninterrupted. Since most of us are on vacation, I thought this venue would be most practical. By the way, I spoke to Jack about his highly negative report and he assured me that in his forthcoming book about American Judaism, there will be a more optimistic review of our movement. In fact, he will underscore some of the newer and creative programs initiated throughout our synagogues to boost attendance and membership."

Aaron Schuster, a Rabbi from New Jersey offered, "I noticed that a Minyan is scheduled in the Card Room at 7:00 P.M. Shall we all attend or continue with our important discussions?"

Milton responded, "It would be risky if we did not attend. Management knows that we are a rabbinic group and we can't ignore a religious service that may reflect negatively on our movement."

"Ira Braun from Boston lamented, "But this Minyan will no doubt be an Orthodox service with men and women separated by a *mechitzah*. I feel uncomfortable attending a service that betrays a fundamental principle of our movement regarding gender equality."

Milton replied, "Your objection Ira is noted, but in this case, inappropriate. First, women do not attend *Ma'ariv*, evening, services so we don't have to be concerned about the *mechitzah*, separation. Second, this is the Catskills, where by tradition, virtually all religious services at Hotels are Orthodox to accommodate the small minority of observant guests who are Orthodox. Those few who are non-Orthodox and attend to say *Kaddish* are sympathetic and respectful, not hostile, to Orthodoxy."

Sarah Kassner, a Rabbi from Brooklyn, raised the question, "Shall I attend? I feel most uncomfortable to participate in a gender–segregated service. No, I will not sit behind a partition."

Milton answered, "Your objection is understandable, Sarah, but as Conservative Jews we have always been pragmatic and willing to compromise when it is for the sake of peace."

Sarah argued, "Then I shall not attend these services which I find compromising to my fundamental belief in women's equality."

Milton continued, "So noted, Sarah."

"But can't we have our own Minyan here in this room? We can ask a few guests to join us for a Minyan," Ira suggested.

Milton answered, "That will make matters even worse. It will appear that we reject the fellowship of our Orthodox neighbors."

"I agree with you," said Sarah. "I think I can forego some of my ideals for a day."

"You are on solid Halakhic grounds, Sarah. Our Talmudic sages sometimes made a temporary *takanah,* reform, in order to maintain peace. Let's proceed with our urgent business regarding the *Report.*"

"We all agree with your sage advice, Milton," said Ira.

"LET ME BEGIN this conference with a personal observation," said Milton. "I was deeply shaken after reading the Report. I can hardly believe that one of our own venerable professors at our beloved Seminary has produced such a scathing and depressing Report about the state of Conservative Judaism."

Ira Braun replied, "Depressing? I think it was disheartening and blasphemous! Not even the Satmar Rebbe could have expressed such offensive remarks about our movement. I've lived my entire life as a loyal and faithful Conservative Jew and hope to do so until I die."

Sarah suggested, "Depressing or blasphemous, we first have to evaluate the validity and accuracy of the Report. Personally, I believe our dear professor has a bias against liberal Judaism and would prefer that we turn the clock back and return to the *shtetl* way of life, which was tradition *without* change."

Aaron Schuster suggested, "I think we should outline the basic conclusions of the Report and evaluate them one by one, rather than evaluating the Report as a whole."

"Splendid idea, Aaron," Milton said. "And what do you think, Max?"

Max Schwartzman was the youngest of the group and was a member of the Seminary faculty - not a pulpit Rabbi. He offered, "Frankly, I see no shocking crisis in our movement. The Report, though most critical, was fair and accurate. It aligns Jewish society which is mostly liberal today, with similar trends in Christian America. Liberal Protestant Churches are declining and Evangelical Churches are growing. Liberal Judaism, including our movement, is declining and Orthodox Judaism is growing. Our movement's so-called *crisis* is neither surprising nor alarming. It's a natural response to the changing social realities of our age."

Milton responded sharply, "Natural or not, our steep decline in membership is a horrendous crisis. The decrease in our congregational membership by thirty per cent this past decade, has led more than one hundred of our member congregations to close their doors or merge with others. Fewer congregations mean fewer Rabbis are needed. Fewer Rabbis needed places our Seminary Rabbinical School at risk. Did you know that less than one hundred students entered the freshman year of all the liberal Rabbinical Seminaries put together? That's less than some of the minor Yeshivas in Brooklyn! Now that is a horrifying crisis!"

THE FIVE selected to constitute this select committee reflected the diversity of the Conservative Rabbinate. Milton Golden, retired for more than five years, was one of the leading ideologues of Conservative Judaism. After a successful forty-year career in Long Island, and having authored numerous outstanding works on biblical scholarship, his appointment to head this Blue Ribbon committee was uncontested. A former Chairman of the Committee on Jewish Laws and Standards, many regarded him as an Elder Statesman and the most authoritative voice of Conservative Judaism. He was often chosen to be the keynote speaker at national conventions and conferences.

Milton Golden's powerful orations at rabbinic conventions were influential in smoothly steering the movement through a number of hotly-debated and controversial issues by negotiating an acceptable compromise regarding: Women's equality and ordination, same-sex marriage and acceptance of Gays and Lesbians.

BORN in Brooklyn, Milton was deeply rooted in traditional Judaism. As a youth, he attended the Orthodox Yeshiva, Torah Vodaath, and then entered the Teacher's Institute of Yeshiva University in upper Manhattan where he graduated with honors. Like other children of immigrants, he felt dissatisfied with the rigid, archaic, atmosphere of the Orthodox schools. Upon graduation from Yeshiva College at the top of his class, he enrolled in the more liberal and modern Jewish Theological Seminary, the fountainhead of Conservative Judaism.

Moses Golden, Milton's father, was a kosher butcher, and strict adherent of Orthodox Judaism who had studied in a Yeshiva in Kovno, Lithuania. He was most distressed, and disappointed in his son's decision to leave the Orthodox yeshiva. He believed that Milton, an outstanding Talmudic scholar, was being groomed to be a *Rosh Yeshiva*, Dean.

He lamented, "Moishele, my son, I cannot believe that after fifteen years of study at the leading yeshivas, you are throwing away your life by forsaking our Orthodox faith. We Jews survived because we observed all the customs and commandments, great and small, without change or compromise to be like the *Goyim*, like the Reform and Conservatives. My heart is bleeding. I feel ashamed to go to shul and face my Rebbe. Please, I beg you, reconsider your decision. Think carefully what you are doing to our family and its reputation. My father was a respected *Dayan* in Kovno. I doubt that my present customers will consider me trustworthy to operate a kosher meat market."

Milton was not surprised by his father's critical reaction. "Tateh, Tateh, I will never betray you or do anything to shame your name. I will always love and respect you and our traditions. But I must be truthful to my beliefs. I cannot remain in the Orthodox Yeshiva. I must follow my genuine beliefs and seek Torah in a new way."

His mother, Rivka, a practical and wise woman, encouraged her son's decision.

She appealed to her husband, "Moishele must make his own decision. He is American-born and understands the modern world. The world of immigrant Jews like us must give way to the future. We must continue to love him like before."

But Milton's decision was not without a deep inner torment and anxiety. In addition to his Talmudic studies at the Orthodox yeshivas, he had also studied the writings of the great modern Jewish scholars of central Europe of the past century who produced scholarly works which traced the history and development of the Bible and Talmud. They revealed the dynamic and changing character of Judaism and how it modified and adjusted to conflicting civilizations. The belief in an unchanging Orthodoxy of his father was no longer a viable choice for him. We in America, he believed, must similarly modernize and adjust our synagogues and faith to American norms.

Milton felt that his father's Orthodoxy would disappear in America within a generation. A new Judaism that was vibrant and dynamic was inevitable. A faith that tries to resist change was bound to crumble. No, he had to leave the yeshiva world for a more open and modern faith. His decision to abandon the yeshiva was encumbered with an unsettled heart. It not only breached the peace and harmony of his family but created an inner turmoil in his soul that could not be totally pacified.

Added to his personal turmoil, a number of dear and close classmates from the yeshiva avoided him. They called him, "traitor" to the faith of Orthodoxy and particularly to his family. He was abandoning a time-tested ancient faith for a voguish fad. He was renouncing his loyalty to his school, friends and shul.

But other classmates secretly admired his courage to follow his own mind and heart and make a dauntless change. They, too, sensed that Orthodoxy was dying in America - Conservative Judaism represented the future. Many new Conservative synagogues, Americanized and modern, were being launched rapidly in the suburbs of New York and other major cities.

And who were the Rabbis of these newly erected large and modern synagogues on Long Island and other suburbs throughout America? More than half were Orthodox Rabbis from the most prestigious yeshivas of America and Europe. They were deeply immersed in the Talmud and traditional texts of Orthodoxy and felt comfortable in the Conservative synagogues which made only minimal changes in the liturgy and synagogue practices.

IRA BRAUN a successful Rabbi in Boston, was born and raised in Philadelphia, a bastion of Conservative Judaism, which flourished when he was a youth. He attended Graetz College Hebrew High School, following eight years in a Day School and three summers in Ramah Camps. He was thoroughly committed to, and confident with, the ideology of his movement and its future - though most saddened to note its recent decline both in his home -town and throughout America.

What was needed under the present crisis, he believed, was more modernization to attract the third and fourth generations of assimilated American Jews who were successful and highly educated. They were professionals, academicians, and most significant - intermarried couples. Greater outreach to intermarried couples was needed to stem the tide of their defection to Reform Judaism.

In fact, he was convinced that members of his rabbinic group ought to be allowed to attend the weddings of the children of his congregants who were being intermarried. He circulated a clandestine petition among his closest colleagues to propose a change in the by-laws of his organization. Some of the older veteran rabbis attacked his proposal as blasphemous and an egregious offense against the

Halakha and the very foundations of their movement. He mused; *change* is tough and challenging to our older colleagues, but imperative to survive and flourish

A GRADUATE of the Reconstructionist Rabbinical Seminary, Sarah Kassner had chosen the Rabbinate as a second career after ten years as a public school teacher. Divorced and living with her friend, Marianne, and her out of wedlock two-year old daughter, she was the first open Lesbian to be admitted to her rabbinic group. After her divorce and decision to be an open Lesbian, she was rejected by her own parents, both children of immigrants from Poland, and alienated from most of her relatives and friends. She eventually found comfort and a secure place in a newly-established Temple in Manhattan that welcomed Jewish Lesbians and Gays.

While her background was minimally traditional - her parents maintained a kosher home, a traditional Passover Seder and attended services on the High Holidays at a neighborhood Orthodox shul in the Bronx. Her experience of a warm welcome and acceptance at her new synagogue for Gays and Lesbians inspired her belief in Judaism. After studying for three years at the Reconstructionist Seminary, she was ordained.

She loved her new career and the open tent, sense of inclusion and diversity of Conservative Judaism that enabled her to fulfill her deepest emotional cravings for meaning and happiness. Unlike others in the committee, she saw no serious crisis in the movement. The declining numbers did not portend a refutation of their ideology or an inevitable dissolution of their group, but the opportunity to be smaller, more committed and idealistic. She mused: Consider the fact that Jesus had only ten loyal devotees who became the foundation of a world–wide faith. No, there was no need to offer any new radical changes or solutions for their movement. She was happy, comfortable and fulfilled - despite the present negative trend. The pessimistic conclusions of the Report should be rejected.

MAX SCHWARTZMAN, a faculty member at the Seminary, had authored numerous books on Jewish theology and wrote the standard history of Conservative Judaism. He strongly opposed the renowned sociologist, Marshall Sklare, who exposed the true origins of Conservative Judaism in America as a convenient social outgrowth of the migration of second generation Jewish-Americans to the suburbs. It was their quest for a more Americanized and comfortable institution, Sklare asserted - not religious belief - that rejected their immigrant-Orthodox parents and initiated the Conservative movement.

But Schwartzman argued that the origins of Conservative Judaism in America had its spiritual roots in the great revolution of Jewish scholarship in central Europe in the last century called *Judische Wissenschaft*. It was modern Jewish scholarship - not social convenience, - that laid the foundation of Conservative Judaism in America.

Max had a minimal Jewish education as a youth, but became attracted to religion during his college days at the Hillel meetings. A deeply committed rationalist, he became a devotee of Professor Mordecai Kaplan who advocated a scientific view of Judaism without supernaturalism, called *Reconstructionism.* "God" to Kaplan, was an idea created by man to further his own ideals and salvation - and not a supernatural, transcendent being.

Max was not conflicted by the numerous academic and scientific challenges to the Bible or Talmudic tradition. The Jewish religion, he believed, was a product of imperfect mortals, not of a supernatural and infallible Deity, and reflected the level of human culture in each generation. If the

Report exposed the flaws and egregious blunders of his religious movement, it was time to make the necessary adjustments – evolutionary change - not radical reform - as the essence of historic Judaism and the key to its survival and flourishing.

AARON SCHUSTER was a native of Toronto and received an intensive Jewish and Hebraic education from the city's well-organized and admirable Day Schools through High School level. He had served in a congregation in New Jersey for more than thirty years. A son of Polish Holocaust survivors, he was deeply committed to Jewish survival and continuity throughout the Diaspora but believed that Aliyah to Israel was the most viable and ultimate solution to the problem of the diminishing Jewish population.

Unlike many of his American colleagues, he strongly experienced the woeful memory of the Holocaust that was palpable in Toronto. Despite the great sense of freedom and tolerance in his homeland and in America, there was a lingering suspicion that *It* could happen here. He and his wife had already purchased a condo in Jerusalem where he spent his vacations and where he hoped to retire in a few years.

Charles H. Freundlich

AARON declared, "I'm not surprised or shaken up by the horrendous Report about the future of non-Orthodox Judaism in America. It was to be anticipated despite the flourishing period of our movement in the previous generation. What we are witnessing in this generation is a tidal wave of social disintegration more devastating than the challenges that confronted our people in Europe at the beginning of the Emancipation and Enlightenment. I am referring to the present disintegration of a Judeo-Christian ethos in America and Europe, the spread of radical individualism, and the cult of the sovereign self. In a nutshell, the powerful social currents that have dominated the present generation militate against any form of committed community endeavor and especially to traditional Judaism in the synagogue.

"It is only in the traditional home and family where some rituals of personal choice like the Seder, and where the ethos of individualism, and the sovereign-self holds sway, is there manifest a hope for Jewish communal practice and the survival of the synagogue. Jews have become too individualistic, striving for self-fulfillment, to be involved in community engagement. Synagogues require a spirit of inter-dependence and cooperation to be effective.

The Third Mountain

"In addition to the social challenges throughout western civilization, there are the particular challenges of the Conservative synagogue: its formal worship services in Hebrew, a foreign language, obedience to a distant and abstract God-idea or God-power, and to any form of obligatory values or so-called *mitzvo*s, commandments – which are so distressing and unacceptable to this generation. Our synagogue movement cannot thrive in this social current without totally rethinking the traditions and values both in the Bible, Talmud and the Halakha!

"I might add two important facts: First, the fact that we are losing numerous members to Reform Judaism, a movement that has replaced us as the largest in our country; and second, that there is hardly any difference in the character, observance and identity between the congregants of our movement and those in liberal Reform. Both are highly secular and marginal to Jewish organizational life and committed synagogue attendance. I heard from a distinguished colleague a few years ago during a New Jersey Board of Rabbis meeting, that it was time for the merger of both the Conservative and Reform movements which comprise identical congregants."

RABBI GOLDEN was shaken. "I can't believe that an experienced long-time and dedicated colleague, like you, Aaron, would call for an end to our movement. It would be a sad and tragic day for Judaism and our Seminary and I will devote every fiber of my body and soul to fight this insidious idea. I've given the best years of my life to our Conservative ideals and movement. I will never agree to this shocking idea. Shame on you!"

Aaron apologized gently, "I meant no disrespect, Milton. I admire your scholarship and rabbinic experience. No other voice in the last half-century has been more powerful, articulate and influential than yours, in advancing the philosophy of our movement. Your numerous scholarly works on the Bible and other works outlining a faith for moderns are legendary. But the declining numbers of our movement - the loss of one quarter of a million members, the loss and merger of many of our synagogues - reflects a radical change in the thinking and beliefs of this generation."

IRA added his voice to the plan of merger with Reform. "We have to face the sorrowful facts, Milton. You began your career in the 50's when one hundred new Conservative synagogues were being launched each year. Those were the halcyon days of our movement and we became the largest in America. Our pews were filled with a core of faithful and traditional Jews. Who were they? Some were immigrants from Eastern Europe, mostly from *shtetls;* others were Holocaust survivors, who were infused with Jewish traditions, holiday observances and most of all, Jewish literacy, to read and appreciate the Hebrew prayers. They had Jewish souls, a deep sense of Jewish identity – call it *tribalism*- and they only married Jews. They are long gone, mostly dead. We are left with marginal Jews who have not filled their places."

AARON concurred, "Our present synagogues are now empty of those congregants nurtured by the intense Jewish culture of the shtetl. Our present congregants, third and fourth generation Jews, are devoid of passion for Jewish tradition and their souls are hollow. Our Conservative synagogues with their mostly Hebrew liturgy are alien to their ethos and culture. Is it no wonder that Reform Judaism has inherited twenty per cent of our membership, while ten percent of today's Orthodoxy is a gift from our finest, most educated and committed youth - graduates of Day Schools and Camp Ramah? The facts are clear, Milton. The ideological program of our movement: Liberalization, Innovation, and

Beautification, has failed – failed to increase more observance of Jewish tradition among our membership or attract a new younger generation to our ranks."

IRA added, "I was raised in Philly with a very dynamic and flourishing Conservative movement. Our synagogue buildings were models of great architecture and beauty. Our Hebrew schools were first-rate, a reflection of a vibrant Hebrew Board of Education. Our pews were filled both on Friday nights and Shabbat mornings. Our U.S.Y. groups were exciting, dynamic and inspiring.

"Then we experienced the inevitable - a traumatic exodus to the suburbs, similar to other American cities. Gradually our congregations declined and our shuls - magnificent wonders of architecture - were sold.

"Liberalization failed because the third generation of Jews were already assimilated, politically liberal, and did not need a synagogue to impress them with what they already believed.

"Innovation failed because they already enjoyed a full array of modern cultural amenities from T.V. to the computer, to the smart phone, to satisfy their needs and did not need new gimmicks.

"Beautification failed because Jews were

already affluent, thoroughly assimilated, flourishing and became the new WASPS, the cultural elite in academia, politics, finance and the arts. The women dressed in trendy fashions, and men drove the latest and most expensive cars. They relocated to the most exclusive suburbs and lived in the most opulent homes. We need less tradition, and more change!

"I'm with Aaron. Why not merge with our Reform colleagues in establishing one great and united *Progressive Judaism?"*

MILTON spoke, his voice quivering, "I'd like to hear from you Sarah, the youngest of our committee.

Sarah responded, "I must admit that I am reluctant to express my opinion in the presence of so many erudite veteran rabbis. I assume that I was chosen because you required diversity and I was the only Lesbian available."

Milton objected, "Not true, Sarah. We examined your record and articles in the Brooklyn Press and we are proud of your achievements. You were selected because you bring a new and fresh voice to our movement. Please feel free to express your opinion as a rabbi - not as a woman or a Lesbian."

Charles H. Freundlich

SARAH began, "As you know, I was not brought up in a traditional Jewish home and received no Hebrew education as a youth and I did not have a Bat Mitzvah. My parents were minimally observant – we had a kosher home – in deference to my grandparents who also lived in the Bronx. The shul my parents attended on the High Holidays was Orthodox, though most of the people there, like my parents, were not Sabbath observers. My parents did not believe that a girl needed a Jewish education and I was discouraged from taking Hebrew language courses when I attended James Monroe High School.

"But, I was loved very much by my grandparents and learned about their many traditional customs that were typical of the shtetl. They spoke to me in Yiddish, which I hardly knew, but felt in my heart, and was told stories of their religious life in the shtetl before they came to America. I sometimes spent a weekend in their home and enjoyed the Sabbath meal and the singing of the traditional *zemirot.*

"But my parents were Socialists and only tolerant of a few Jewish observances. After my divorce, I decided to *come out* and reveal my life as a Lesbian and live with a friend and my daughter. As a single mother, I was unhappy with my career as a teacher in the public school system in which I spent ten years. I felt a void in my life and sought to fill it with a change in career or perhaps moving to a smaller community.

"By chance, I noticed an article in the Jewish Week about a new synagogue in Manhattan that was being formed to serve the Gays and Lesbians. I attended and felt that a weight was lifted from my heart while in the presence so many others, like me, who had been rejected by friends and family. I found the services somewhat challenging, but the warmth of the congregation convinced me that I was home. I took an interest in learning Hebrew and eventually attended the Reconstructionist Seminary which was welcoming to Gays and Lesbians. I have been with my congregation in downtown Brooklyn for three years and am most satisfied.

"Now to the issue at hand: how shall we respond to the infamous Report? First, let me admit that before I became a Rabbi, I, as a Lesbian, was part of a small excluded community. Numbers or size did not matter to me. Thus, the declining number in our movement is not significant. I do not fear the total disappearance of our movement within decades.

"Just consider the number of existing congregations - over five hundred - with their rabbis, teachers, custodians, Presidents, Sisterhoods and

Brotherhoods - who are active. They have a personal stake in the survival of these synagogues, the congregants and the buildings. Though individuals may drop out, institutions acquire a life of their own.

"In numerous smaller towns, these synagogues, though not well attended, provide legitimacy and status amidst the larger Gentile population. Above all, they provide both friendly communal adhesion and stature for the Jewish individual. The Jew is never alone or powerless when he or she is a member of a synagogue community.

"The Report has created a hysterical reaction of a doomsday for our movement. I prefer to see our present strength and vitality for years to come. No, we do not need any radical change or a merger with Reform, another movement which is similarly challenged."

MILTON was most gratified with Sarah's views. "And what does our distinguished professor of Jewish theology have to add that will be positive and allow us to begin dinner?"

Max had been silently meditating about his personal views which might be offensive to his colleagues. He was first and foremost a scholar, fully committed to life-long learning and his home was the Seminary and its magnificent library - not the synagogue. The other Rabbis were involved with servicing their congregants, most of whom were *am ha-aratzim*, ignoramuses, who attended their synagogues rarely and joined as a matter of ethnic and community convenience. Theology, the worship of God, and the serious study of Torah, were alien to most congregants and their culture. The decline of the number of Conservative Synagogues was not a major loss for the survival of the Conservative ideology and unique Torah scholarship.

The Seminary was the main epicenter of Conservative Judaism - not the numerous synagogues. It, alone, was the citadel of modern Jewish scholarship and the heart of historic Judaism. As long as the Seminary with its faculty of world-class scholars in Talmud, Bible and Literature was thriving, and was well-endowed and a magnet to attract serious students, the ideology of Conservative Judaism was not threatened but assured for the future.

MAX began: "My dear colleagues. I have a personal confession to make. I don't really give a damn about the decline in the number of synagogues in our movement. Most of our congregants are neither well-informed nor loyal to our conservative faith. Perhaps they would be better off by joining Reform Temples with its minimum of Hebrew liturgy, obligation or commitment to traditional rituals and its total autonomy to choose or discard their way of Judaism.

"We still maintain a Jewish Committee of Laws and Standards, with its conflicting decisions that confuse rather than illuminate. Our congregants hardly know that Conservative Judaism has laws or standards. They are free to do what they want, just like the members of Reform Temples. Just try and demand that they commit to our laws and standards! Are we not deceiving ourselves? Have we not already violated the boundaries of Halakha in our quest for modernization and accommodation to a new and unrestrained sexual culture, alien to our Torah and tradition?

"I am not disturbed by the radical changes in our movement. I have never believed in a supernatural God that commands, punishes or rewards human behavior. Nor do I believe that a supernatural God speaks to man and has given us a divine Torah. Our Seminary professors have long taught the Bible and the Talmud as historic, dynamic and developing works of fallible human beings, not divinely inspired works to be obeyed. The biblical

stories of our Patriarchs and Moses are myths –
inspiring - but neither true nor divine.

"Given this secular-humanistic approach, who
needs worship in a synagogue to a God or faith in
Torah that nobody believes? If our own Seminary
rabbinical graduates are devoid of a faith in a
personal God who reveals a Torah, commands,
demands, rewards and punishes, heals and enlightens
and redeems – how can they inspire their own
congregants or a new generation of congregants to
be inspired, faithful or committed to a synagogue or
faith without God?

"I believe that we should develop a new
smaller movement of Jews concentrated around our
Seminary, who would be committed to life-long
learning of Torah and the fellowship of other
scholars. This fellowship may well develop into a
new movement based on learning as a spiritual
ideal."

MILTON agreed, "You know, Max, you have
an interesting point. It is quite possible that the first
institution for a prayer service in Babylon, called a
Bet Haknesset, synagogue, included a lecture on a
portion of the Torah reading, called a Midrash. Later
another institution called a Bet Hamidrash was
created to emphasize Torah-study which may also

have included prayer services. Nevertheless, the status of the Bet Hamidrash was deemed higher in holiness than that of a Bet Haknesset – learning Torah was a greater mitzvah than praying. Perhaps we should be converting our synagogues into Houses of Study? The classical rabbi was a scholar-teacher not a preacher-pastor."

MAX noted that it was time for dinner and all agreed. "Later, we can attend this evening's show in the Playhouse. I understand that it features a famous Cantor from Brooklyn offering both Broadway hits and Yiddish favorites."

Milton apologized, "You will excuse my not joining you for this evening's show, but I am exhausted from the drive from Long Island. We have had a most fruitful meeting. I have recorded our various views and will work on a written summary in the early morning for tomorrow's meeting after breakfast."

MILTON felt apprehensive that evening and tossed in his bed trying to sleep. He was deeply perturbed by the thought of merging with Reform Judaism.

He reflected on the course of his lengthy rabbinical career: Did not his four colleagues know the significant merit of our movement founded on history and Halakha? Reform had already abolished the binding character of the Halakha, the rituals of the Bible, Kashrut and the Temple. In contrast, Conservative Judaism had preserved the Shabbat the Holidays, the laws of Kashrut and especially the centrality of Hebrew in the prayer services. How could there be a merger?

Hardly three years after the infamous *treife banquet* for the graduates of the Cincinnati Reformers - Rabbi Sabato Morais and Rabbi Henry Periera Mendes, two leading Sephardic Orthodox Rabbis, reacted and established our Seminary in 1886. It was later to become the fountainhead of Conservative Judaism in America.

My young colleagues are not going *forward* with their idea of a merger, but *backwards!* They disregard the ten percent of our congregants who observe a measure of Jewish tradition and would never adjust to the liberal Reform movement. Where would they go? Certainly not to Orthodoxy which is becoming more extreme, beyond the levels of the European shtetls. No, we must preserve our movement for the thousands who have thrived in it.

But am I thinking clearly?

Who are my colleagues?

Charles H. Freundlich

Many of the rabbis, like me, who chose the Conservative movement, were nurtured in Orthodox yeshivas and were *molei v'gadush*, totally immersed, in Talmud and the *Shulhan Arukh*. They struggled thirty to forty hours a week swimming in the Sea of the Talmud, in its intricate dialectics, in Rashi and Tosafot. They had to master the laws of Kashrut in the *Yoreh Deah* with the profound commentaries of the *Taz* and the *Shach*. They provided legitimacy and status to the Conservative synagogues which had made minimal changes in the *siddur*.

An Orthodox-educated Rabbi who chose to serve in a Conservative pulpit, like many of my friends, might still feel at home, by rationalizing – there was a need for a comfortable place for moderately observant Jews – a middle path between Orthodoxy and Reform, lest they stop attending, and become alienated completely from Judaism. These Orthodox Rabbis in Conservative pulpits were manning the fortifications of Jewish tradition against the tidal wave of assimilation and indeed were the guardians of authentic Judaism in these new synagogues.

But now, who are my Conservative colleagues? What do they know of intensive studies of Talmud, or of Halakha? They are mostly novices who barely touched the surface of Jewish studies like spoiled college students. They do not have passion or deep commitment to Torah or God. They are skilled professionals, functionaries, serving their congregants' need for feeling good and secure in their secular-ethnic Judaism!

God is not in our synagogues! How, then, can we serve Him?

"Tateh, Tateh, what have I done?"

Charles H. Freundlich

THE LIONESS

Charles H. Freundlich

The Third Mountain

WILTONBURY, a small town in Connecticut, was no different than others in New England with its small group of powerful elites. Needless to say, the Jewish community had its own group of *machers*, elites, often the richest, most philanthropic and outspoken. Mostly, they were the owners of large and lucrative retail, furniture or clothing businesses that employed numerous other Jews therefore wielding considerable leverage and control. They also included highly successful physicians, attorneys and judges who were well-regarded by the general community. This group of Jews was the backbone and the visible symbol that bestowed legitimacy and respectability vis-a-vis the majority deeply-rooted and entrenched Christian gentry.

In Wiltonbury, the reach and celebrity of a number of these notables was national. One became the national President of Conservative Synagogues, while another member of a liberal synagogue became the President of Hadassah, the largest women's organization in the world.

This is the story of Freda Steiner of the renowned Steiner family, owners of *Steiners Furniture*, exclusive dealers of Thomasville and other fine furniture, who were among the most distinguished of the Jewish nobility. Freda's husband, Howard, was the third generation to operate the successful furniture establishment after his grandfather, Moses Steiner, an immigrant from Lithuania, opened a dry goods shop in the downtown section of Wiltonbury.

While Howard was preoccupied with managing his large furniture enterprise, his wife, Freda, was equally engaged with numerous charitable activities in the poorer sections of Wiltonbury, in addition to Jewish causes like Beth El Synagogue, Israel Bonds, UJA and Hadassah. She was also a member of the Board of Directors of the city's United Fund and the YMCA.

Freda was not only a *macher* - she was a passionate liberal voice in a mostly conservative society. When the new building of Beth El was planned, it was Freda who insisted that the school wing include a large gymnasium and basketball court, which would be open to the general community, at least one evening a week. This demanded an addition of a hundred thousand dollars. But Freda assured the Building Committee that she would personally raise the money, and she did. Her husband was her strongest ally.

Howard questioned her, "Darling you know that our own Jewish children do not need an additional gymnasium; they have one in public school. Are you doing this for the poorer element in the general community?"

Freda countered, "Howard, a gym at Beth El will bring the Jewish children together with non-Jewish children and help develop mutual understanding. But mostly, Jewish children will socialize with other Jewish children, play together and eventually will date each other and perhaps marry each other."

"I know you are right, darling. But you know that our family will end up footing most of the bill."

"I love you Howard for your uncompromising support and understanding."

The most contentious of Freda's proposals was to open up a Soup Kitchen in the synagogue Vestry for the members of the mostly-needy Black community, every Friday afternoon.

The President, Morris Krieger lamented, "A Soup Kitchen in our beautiful Vestry? The *Shvartzes,* Black*s,* will wreck our building."

Freda countered, "Reverend Smith will be coming with his Deacons and help with the tasks of serving, clean up, and preparing packages of food to take home. Also, Mr. Krieger, I resent your use of the term, *Shvartze*s instead of Blacks. You forget that when your Russian grandparents came to Wiltonbury, not too long ago, they were called, *Kike*s."

While the Board of Directors defeated her proposal, it agreed to a compromise. The congregation would allocate three thousand dollars in its annual budget to the Soup Kitchen located in Rev. Smith's Second African Baptist Church.

When the Dedication Journal for the new building of Beth El was published, it included a pictorial history of the congregation from its earliest days, to the mid-century. Freda Steiner's photo appeared in more than seven important committees, including the School Committee, and Sisterhood.

At home, Howard would note, "Darling you seem very engrossed in your reading. Is it an interesting novel?"

"Interesting? Yes," she responded. "It's the latest book by Rabbi Robert Gordis, *A Faith for Moderns*."

"I've heard of him, a famous Rabbi and distinguished biblical scholar. He gave the main address at our last convention of the United Synagogue in Boston."

"I've learned so much from this book. Gordis writes that many traditional beliefs can be understood and appreciated with a modern interpretation. One can embrace traditional religious faith and scientific truth at the same time."

"I would love to hear some of the interesting ideas," Howard said.

"One idea concerns Revelation – the words of God communicated to prophets. I often wondered how some verses of the Bible could be considered literal words of a perfect supernatural God. The author believes that Revelation is not static, but a dynamic idea. The prophet is a child of a particular socio-historical milieu and hears the words of God according to the limits of his time and environment.

It is our task today to bring our own highest values to understand the ancient words. In other words, Revelation is a cooperative experience between a supernatural God and a finite man. Man and God are partners."

Howard agreed, "I like that idea. I can now understand why some ideas of the Bible which I found unethical and unacceptable – like the mandate to kill all the Canaanites and the burning of witches – were based on an antiquated understanding of the rules of war and society. These ideas are not acceptable today and are not binding on us. Our own understanding of human rights is more humane and ethical."

Freda continued, "I also finished another very enlightening book by Rabbi Abraham Joshua Heschel, *The Sabbath*. I know you will find it truly amazing."

Howard agreed, "I'm delighted that you've advanced your knowledge and understanding of Judaism. Unfortunately, I stopped my formal studies of Judaism when I became a Bar Mitzvah."

Freda continued, "I'm not more learned than you. I had a minimum Jewish education and only attended a Yiddish *Sholom Aleichem School* for a few years – my parents believed that the religious Hebrew School of the synagogue was only for boys.

I learned most of my knowledge of Judaism as a child from observing my parents. My father was moderately Orthodox and he, too, learned many of our customs and ceremonies by observing his own parents from the *shtetl*. But these observances were folk customs, not learned laws, based on a true understanding of spiritual values.

"Rabbi Heschel presents a profound and uplifting interpretation of the Sabbath in his book. Sabbath is holiness in *time,* not space. You might call it a transformative experience for me. I've been lighting candles every Friday evening mechanically without any in-depth understanding. I wish you would find time to read some of these books, Howard. Then we could both grow more spiritually together."

"Darling, you know how hectic my business schedule is. My life in business is tough and competitive, not spiritual. However, I promise that I will try to find some time to begin reading some of your books."

"Promise?"

"I promise to make a small start."

WHILE HER DAILY routine was filled with many meetings, Freda devoted much time to advancing her knowledge of Judaism. She felt disappointed that most of the congregants of Beth El were *Conservative Jews* in name only. Only a small minority attended Sabbath services regularly and though a few maintained kosher homes, they all ate non-kosher, *treif,* outside. Though not Orthodox herself, she felt it imperative to be well-informed in all customs, ancient and current, about traditional Judaism. She had majored in English Literature at City College and also took a particular interest in the classical writings of Greece and Rome.

Howard took pride in Freda's numerous communal activities. As a Steiner, he, like his father and grandfather, had been a President of Beth El and remained one of the major-givers. At supper time, Howard would ask, "Well, dear, you look joyous. What battles have we been fighting today?"

Freda was an iconoclast and her powerful feelings about fairness, social justice and the preservation of traditional Jewish life in Wiltonbury often provoked conflict with some of the other progressive elements in the community.

FREDA set boundaries for her liberal pursuits especially when they were in conflict with Jewish traditions. One was the proposal to extend equal roles to women during the worship services. A new trend in many synagogues was counting women as part of the *Minyan*, the necessary quorum of ten men, for communal prayer, and especially for the chanting of the *Kaddish* memorial prayer.

Sarah Kigel, the Sisterhood President, had argued at a recent meeting, to approach the Ritual Committee to allow women full equality in all religious services. The proposal appeared to gather the support of the entire Sisterhood Board, and a vote was about to be held by the general board.

Freda, however, raised her hand in opposition to the proposal. When given the floor, she stood up and with compelling words asserted her strong objection: "I think this proposal is both offensive and destructive to family harmony. I feel that when my husband, Howard, receives an *Aliyah*, honor, to the Torah, I want to share and support his moment of recognition and joy as his wife. I would never want to be honored with an Aliyah to the Torah while my husband is sitting in the audience. I have a role as a partner and not as a competitor. I am engaged in many activities that afford me both prestige and personal satisfaction. The *Minyan* and the *Aliyot* are two ancient rituals that bestow honor and status to men. They are precious because they are exclusive for men. Ladies, let's not start a sex-war in which we all will lose."

Mrs. Kigel was startled and countered, "I can't believe that in this age you, Freda, a committed liberal, still has to feel subservient to your husband. Women have taken their role as equals throughout all modern societies. Times have changed. We women must demand equality in all synagogue matters."

Mrs. Rosen, the secretary, then voiced her opinion: "Like most of the women in this congregation, I don't attend Sabbath services regularly or am I counted in the *Minyan*, which I do not attend, or even receive an *Aliyah*. This is not important to me or my husband. In fact, to be honest, most of us here do not attend services regularly on the Sabbath. I think the small group of traditional, dedicated men who do attend the services regularly would be just as happy without any changes in the services."

Mrs. Kigel responded, "I didn't think that I was stirring up a hornet's nest with so much heated controversy. I think we should table this discussion for a while until we do a little more research. We have enough problems and challenges. I mean, with many of our married children going through a divorce and are alienated from the synagogue and others intermarrying, I think we have enough conflicts."

As usual, the judgment of Freda was enough to sway the majority.

Mrs. Kigel whispered to Mrs. Rosen, "It seems that any opinion of Freda, no matter how inappropriate, carries more weight than the whole Board of Sisterhood."

Mrs. Rosen responded, "That's because Freda is not only married to a macher, she herself, is a Lioness."

FREDA'S MOST noteworthy and courageous confrontation dealt with the controversy over the tenure of Rabbi Herman Epstein, who had served Beth El for more than thirty years. Over the course of his tenure, Rabbi Epstein had cultivated a number of powerful enemies. Most of the conflicts dealt with minor issues of ritual and the Rabbi's traditional views. Freda and Howard were staunch supporters of the Rabbi and his traditional ideals.

Freda lamented, "I don't understand why some of our congregants do not appreciate your inspiring sermons and your pastoral visits, Rabbi."

"Freda dear, you may have heard the saying: you can't please them all. A Rabbi who tries to satisfy everyone will end up satisfying no one."

"Well, Rabbi, you can count on Howard and me."

"Thank you. You must remember that some of our congregants are people I would be hestitant to socialize with were I not required to do so as their Rabbi. In addition, quite a number of our congregants are emotionally challenged and feel a burning need to be loved, appreciated and noticed. And some of the women who have no careers, but have lots of time as homemakers, find life dull and look to me to fill their hearts with meaning. I try to do my best, Freda. But for some congregants, that's not enough."

"Rabbi, I'm sure there are many, many congregants who admire your efforts and your activities throughout the Jewish and non-Jewish community."

"I try to follow my best instincts and the traditions of Judaism and of my dear parents. I refuse to wear a black robe during services because it is an imitation of the Christian Church attire. That irks some of our highly-assimilated congregants who think that I am simply a Jewish priest."

RABBI EPSTEIN let it be known that he would not attend a wedding or Bar Mitzvah celebration if it was not kosher. The Social Hall at Beth El was kosher and capacious but it was not decorous or luxurious and it could only seat two hundred and fifty guests. Anita Green, a non-Jewish caterer handled most of the synagogue affairs. Congregants wishing a more exclusive affair had to invite a Jewish caterer from Hartford, while those having a much larger guest list would schedule their banquet at the Central Hotel in downtown Wiltonbury, which did not have a kosher kitchen.

Rabbi Epstein was adamant in his refusal to attend these non-kosher affairs at the Central Hotel. His personal attendance, he believed, would send the wrong message that a Jewish religious festivity could be held with a non-kosher meal.

Hershel Drinsky, son of Henry Drinsky and grandson of Oscar Drinsky, owner of Drinsky Plumbing Supplies, a founder of Beth El, and a most generous benefactor, was scheduled to celebrate his Bar Mitzvah party at the Central Hotel. This issue became most divisive. The Rabbi's refusal to attend was a slap not only to Oscar Drinsky, a founding *macher*, but to the whole congregation.

It was whispered throughout the congregation that the Rabbi had lost touch with his congregation. The time had come when Rabbi Epstein, aged sixty-four, should be retired!

Freda was disturbed by the malicious gossip regarding the Rabbi. He was neither senile nor estranged from the congregation. Indeed, Freda had become a faithful regular at the Rabbi's Thursday morning Adult Education classes and admired his warmth, sensitivity and scholarship.

President Krieger was deeply disturbed by the fracas over the Drinsky Bar Mitzvah party and it required an immediate resolution. For a long time, Beth El could not sustain itself with the membership dues alone. At the end of the year, it was a small group of four or five wealthy businessmen, including Oscar Drinsky, who made up the deficit of the budget. No way, was Oscar Drinsky to be alienated from his central role as a major-giver and pillar of Beth El.

But would the Rabbi be willing to bend a little – just this one time? How often did Rabbi Epstein serve as the peacemaker to mediate the virulent feuds between the members? Mr. Krieger invited Rabbi Epstein to a *special meeting* of the Executive Committee.

The Rabbi confided in Freda his closest ally, and told her about being invited to the special meeting.

"Well, Freda, do you think that I am too stubborn in my ways? Is it time for me to retire?"

"Of course not, Rabbi. You have many, many friends and admirers. Stick to your principles. Anyway, you can see that I carry a very large leather handbag. You will remember, two years ago, what occurred when I was attacked by a young hoodlum who broke into my home. The newspapers reported that I smacked him so hard that he ran away. What they didn't report was that I smacked him with this large leather handbag that I am now holding. I have also been invited to this special meeting, as a representative of the Sisterhood. I let it be known that I will be coming with my large handbag and the first person that says a nasty word about you will be whacked by me. Oscar Drinsky is not the only macher at Beth El. My husband's grandfather, Moses, also was a founder of Beth El and its first President."

PRESIDENT MORRIS KRIEGER was uneasy and his anxiety was palpable. He began, "Rabbi, I called you to this meeting so that together we can come to some amicable solution for the forthcoming Drinsky Bar Mitzvah party."

"Morris," the Rabbi responded. "You know my views in this matter. I have not attended non-kosher affairs for the past thirty years - since the beginning of my tenure in Beth El. I see no reason to change my views today."

"We do not wish you to compromise your principles, Rabbi. You are profoundly loved and respected throughout Wiltonbury."

"Then what do you want?"

"We want peace and harmony. Some people have noticed that you do eat in a non-kosher establishment."

"That is true. Following morning Minyan, I have my breakfast – a roll, coffee and oatmeal at the Prime Café, downtown. I am often joined by our Cantor who drives downtown. I do not profess to be Orthodox, and am flexible for eating dairy meals."

"So, Rabbi, there is some room for compromise in your observance."

"Freda spoke up, "Rabbi, can you propose a menu that would allow you to attend the Drinsky affair at the Central Hotel?"

"I should be delighted to outline a menu that would not compromise my observance of kashrut. I would be glad to meet with the Drinsky family and their caterer."

A week later, during the meeting, the Rabbi proposed a dairy menu including baked fish. The caterer was shocked. "For baked fish, you don't need an exclusive Catering Hall like the Central Hotel!" he shouted. "No, the standard of the Central Hotel as an exclusive venue would be compromised. Filet mignon, roast beef, stuffed quail would be appropriate – not fish."

Finally, the Rabbi offered a plan that Freda had originally suggested. The caterer should prepare the cuisine in the kosher kitchen of Beth El on Friday and bring it to the Central Hotel before the Sabbath. The dishes of Beth El would also be used. Oscar Drinsky and the Caterer were uncertain.

Then Freda spoke up while waving her handbag, "Oscar, your obstinacy to listen to the Rabbi offends me – offends my family and offends the entire Beth El. You cannot be so inflexible when the Rabbi has offered you a practical and fair solution. In addition, the Rabbi and his wife would be in attendance and offer the opening blessings and proper greetings."

The compromise was accepted. Freda, the Lioness, had achieved victory once again. A nasty congregational dispute had been avoided. The Bar Mitzvah party of Oscar Drinsky's grandson was celebrated joyously and seamlessly. At the close of the dinner, Hershel Drinsky spoke, "I wish to thank you all for coming and sharing my Bar Mitzvah celebration. In particular, I wish to thank Rabbi and Mrs. Epstein for their participation. Their blessings and inspiring words of encouragement will be remembered as I take my place as an adult in Jewish life."

Oscar Drinsky added, "As a founding member of Beth El and its second President, I must add my gratitude to you, Rabbi Epstein, for attending. Your presence added both dignity and honor to this joyous occasion for me, my son Henry and my grandson, Hershel."

THE FOLOWING, month, the Board of Directors voted to retire Rabbi Epstein, appoint him Emeritus, and schedule a gala Testimonial Dinner in his honor. His contract would not be renewed.

EVEN FREDA could not overrule the Board's decision and she was distraught. She said, "Rabbi we are all saddened with the Board's decision. I think that you will always be with us in spirit. Those very special gatherings in your home on Shabbos afternoon to discuss Jewish books and also programs on special days like Tu B'Shevat, Israel Independence Day and Hanukkah, were so meaningful and inspiring. Your *Rebbitsen,* was a warm and loving hostess. We all felt like one family. Too bad, more congregants did not come to your home. But it's their loss.

"Most of all, Rabbi, your warm words and participation at our two sons' Bar Mitzvah will remain in their hearts and our memory. Howard and I always felt uplifted and mesmerized by your heartfelt sermons from the pulpit and scholarly discussions in your home. You and the Rebbitsen will remain our close friends for the rest of our lives."

Rabbi Epstein was visibly shaken. "Freda, it's wonderful that I have dear friends like you and Howard. I consider you and Howard members of my family. We have decided to remain a while in Wiltonbury. After all, this has been our home for more than thirty years. We feel we belong here, even though we were native New Yorkers from Brooklyn."

FREDA felt distressed over the Rabbi's departure. She confessed to Howard, "I think it's time that I withdrew my participation and energies from Beth El. I feel unhappy and unappreciated."

Howard was surprised, "But darling, you have spent almost thirty years in the Sisterhood and other synagogue activities. Beth El has been your home and a major part of your life. They call you, *The Lioness of Wiltonbury*."

Freda responded: "I feel that with our two sons having completed college, married and settled with our grandchildren in Chicago, I have nothing more to do here with so much time. I need a new and more challenging mission to excite me and bring meaning to my life. Do you think I might start a professional career?"

"At fifty-three, you are not too old to begin a Second Act. I will still be occupied in the business and I'll give you all the support – financial and encouragement - that you need."

"I knew you would understand, Howard. I love you so much and I will still be your full partner for every business or social activity you are involved with."

THIRTY YEARS HAD PASSED, and Freda began reflecting on her life in Wiltonbury. Though an outsider, originally from the Bronx, Freda Steiner was considered the premier women's voice in the Jewish community of Wiltonbury. She had met her husband, Howard, in a Singles Weekend in Camp Mohav in the heart of the Catskills, thirty years earlier. Howard had graduated from Yale, and was a Vice-President of his father's well-established furniture business. Freda had recently graduated from City College in New York and was working in sales for a dress manufacturer on 37th Street.

It was serendipity that they met at the tennis courts. She was pretty, slender and wearing a bright blue athletic outfit with a white flower design. Howard approached her. "Mind if I join you?"

Freda noticed Howard's well–built frame and tanned body. It was very enticing. His voice was resounding but pleasing.

"Why not, the court is empty."

Howard's smile was affable and continued, "My name is Howard and I'm from Wiltonbury."

"Wiltonbury? Where's that?"

"In the center of Connecticut. You know, the city with many mills."

"I'm Freda from the Bronx. I assume you have heard of the Bronx."

"Of course, the Yankee Stadium, home of the champions. I've often visited the Bronx with my father to watch the Yankees play."

"I'm not a baseball fan, but we in the Bronx have many other interesting places – the Bronx Zoo, for instance. It's the second largest in the world. What do you do, Howard, when you're not vacationing in the Catskills?"

"I work for my Dad, the owner of Steiners Furniture in Wiltonbury."

Freda felt a little defensive. Was Howard wealthy, in a higher class?

"There are a number of men from the Bronx who are employed in our business. And what do you do?" Howard continued.

"I just graduated from City College as an English-Ed major. I'm working presently as a book-keeper in Manhattan until I can get a job in my field."

They spoke for more than an hour, shared jokes and complained about some of the rudeness of the other guests.

"Can we meet for dinner, and sit together in the Dining Room?"

Howard felt comfortable with Freda. She was diffident and unassuming and was a great listener to his stories about growing up in a small town. Freda felt relaxed and content as she shared her own tales of challenge and desperation growing up in poverty. On Sunday, all the guests would return home.

Howard confessed, "I like you, Freda, from the Bronx. I'd like to see you again. I have a car and it's only two hours from Wiltonbury."

"I enjoyed chatting with you, Howard. You're quite a dancer, too." Freda offered him her phone number.

FREDA'S MOTHER embraced her passionately when she returned home on Sunday evening.

"So did you have a good time in the Catskills? Did you meet a nice boy?"

They sat down in the kitchen.

"Mom, I met someone nice - but I'm scared."

"Darling, let's first eat supper. I made some nice blintzes, and then we'll talk."

"Mom, what concerns me is that this boy I met – very nice, and I like him – comes from a small town, Wiltonbury in Connecticut."

"You mean a *shtetl?* Your father, of blessed memory, and I come from a *shtetl* – so small that after every war it changed its name and nationality.

"That's not all. Howard is a graduate of Yale and from a prominent business family. He presently is a V.P in his father's furniture business. Who am I - a girl from the Bronx, and a child of immigrants, to be so fortunate?"

"Hold on darling. First, you have to remember that your father, of blessed memory was a son of one of the leading families of Horodenka. His father was a man of property with a certification from the Emperor Franz Josef to engage in business. He sat by the Eastern Wall of the Main Synagogue of Horodenka. True, the family lost its property after the World War and the town became part of Poland. Maybe we don't have money now, but we have *yichus,* pedigree, and that is true class and cannot be bought with money. You should always remember the fine family which is your heritage. Your father, of blessed memory, would have been so proud to see you graduate from City College."

"Mom, I believe you, and I understand. But this is America, not Poland, and you cannot have class or *yichus* or pedigree, without money."

"Freda darling, if Howard has real class he will not be a snob. He will see you as a beautiful, kind-hearted and educated young lady and he will love you, and feel honored to share a life with you."

"Mom, I feel a little better. I love you so much and I believe you are right."

HOWARD DATED Freda for the next six Sunday afternoons, attending all the interesting places that she suggested – the Loew's Paradise, Alexander's, Krum's Ice-cream Parlor and the Bronx Zoo. They kissed and Howard felt a great passion to embrace her soft skin, and the warmth of her breath. Freda wondered why this wealthy Yale graduate was attracted to her - a plain girl from the Bronx. She felt he was charming, romantic, stimulating and   energetic. She realized that she was in love. Three months later, they were married.

THE MARRIAGE of an unexceptional girl from the Bronx to a wealthy scion of the Steiners was viewed with some apprehension by the natives who suspected that she was a slick gold digger, way out of her class.

But after six months, Freda was received by the elites and respected. Upon Howard's request, she made monthly trips to New York's fashionable stores, and purchased her wardrobe from Wilma's on 57th Street, where no outfit was less than four hundred dollars. It was Howard's idea that she be dressed stylishly and attain her proper standing among the cream of Jewish society.

But, Freda's newly acquired status was not for show. She was a slim and attractive brunette with an engaging smile to everyone. It was love and joy that motivated her marriage. She also purchased many of her outfits locally because she was more comfortable with a small circle of average women - teachers, social workers and readers of serious books.

She also joined a group of para-chaplains, trained by the local Federation of Charities, to visit the elderly, the sick and lonely and those home-bound. She was not burdened with household chores; Howard had provided a full-time maid to manage their capacious colonial home on Columbia Boulevard. Freda saw this release of routine household chores as an opportunity to give of herself and lead a life of service.

She did not ignore her roots from the Bronx where she had lived in a six-floor brick tenement until her marriage. She continued a close relationship with her old friends and her loving mother and sent her a monthly check. Like Howard, she was not religious, but supported her synagogue and attended services on the High Holidays and special occasions. It was expected that the annual donation of the Steiners, more than ten thousand dollars at the time of *Yizkor,* was well-publicized and influenced the other wealthy congregants to contribute.

Though Freda was not Orthodox, she maintained a kosher home - partly for the sake of her mother who visited often. Also other guests like itinerant Rabbis asking for donations felt welcome and especially because she believed in the power of faith and tradition.

Freda was an avid reader of novels, periodicals and even scholarly works on psychology and politics. The gatherings with her friends for tea at her home enabled her to share her accumulated wisdom of worldly affairs and she became a mentor to many of them.

THE WEALTH of the Steiner family and their record of philanthropy was not lost on the numerous fund-raisers, of local and national institutions and itinerant *shnorers,* beggars, who passed through Wiltonbury. When The Hebrew Day School of New Haven planned its scholarship fund, it was anticipated that Rabbi Hecht, its legendary builder and principal, would call on the Steiners. Rabbi Hecht who boasted a Ph.D. in Education came with his wife, Rivka, to Freda's home with some reservations. He did not usually meet or do business with women.

"I called Mr. Steiner about our Scholarship Fund and he insisted that I meet with you, Mrs. Steiner, the real *boss* of his philanthropic endeavors."

"Howard and I have an arrangement with regard to charitable activities. His work at Steiners Furniture is too demanding to be concerned with daily charitable gifts. I note that you came with Mrs. Hecht and she is welcome."

"Yes, she does the driving. In addition, as a Lubavitcher Hasid I do not meet privately with a woman."

"I understand. I am not Orthodox but I take Judaism very seriously and maintain a kosher home and have accumulated an extensive library of Judaica. I'm so glad to meet you personally, Dr. Hecht – or is it Rabbi Hecht – because your work benefits some of our children in Wiltonbury who attend your Day School."

"I am honored by your gracious words."

"First, let me assure you, Rabbi, that the Steiner Foundation will grant a generous gift to your excellent school. Actually, Rabbi, I was eager to meet with you and have a serious discussion about Judaism. Our Rabbi has recently retired and I miss having a serious personal discussion about religion. Do you have the time now?"

"I certainly have the time to have a serious discussion about Judaism. That is my main mission in life. What are some of your concerns?"

"Let me confess that I admire your Hasidic movement and its excellent work throughout America. Many modern Rabbis wonder at your remarkable success. Your movement defies all that we American Jews believe - to succeed you have to Americanize – in dress, in custom and lifestyle. We non-Orthodox believe this as gospel truth yet we continue to fail. Your members and your *Sheluchim*, Emissaries, do not conform to American mores in dress and culture. All your men have beards, wear black suits, expose their *tsitsis,* fringes, outside their trousers, and your women dress modestly, cover their hair with wigs and eschew much of secular culture. Yet, despite your unconventional ways, you are accepted throughout America and are successful in spreading Judaism. You are the envy of non-Orthodox Rabbis who fail to have any significant influence on their congregants. The question is-why?"

"I'm surprised at your candidness, Mrs. Steiner. Most non-Orthodox Rabbis believe that we Lubavitchers are an anachronism, misfits - with our beards, and black suits and avoidance of modern secular culture and entertainment - most of us do not attend colleges. We are a separate community – not fully integrated or assimilated with American-Jewish society – yet we have succeeded. And I *will* try to explain in a few words how we outsiders have been so successful in touching the hearts and souls of the most secular and irreligious people."

Freda responded, "I suspect, Rabbi, that the answer is revealed in an incident that happened many years ago when I was a youth in the Bronx and attended an Orthodox shul. The shul had engaged a professional Cantor for the blessing of the New Month and for the holidays. Well, this Cantor from

Brooklyn was a Hasid with a beard, long side-curls and wore a *kapote*, a full length frock coat. He had a marvelous voice and thus the modern Orthodox shul overlooked his outmoded ways, and hired him.

"Now here is the remarkable incident that was buried in my mind for many, many years. At the conclusion of the Shabbos morning service, when he davened *Musaf* – he did not stay for the *Kiddush* afterwards, but immediately left the shul. He began his twelve mile, four-hour walk, to return to Brooklyn to spend the afternoon prayer and third meal with his *Rebbe*, especially to sit at his *tish,* table, and share the words of Torah and Shabbos *zemiros*, melodies. We all were astounded by his religious devotion to his *Rebbe* and his commitment to traditional Shabbos afternoon observances. Walking twelve miles from the Bronx to Brooklyn in all kinds of weather!

"Why? Was he a lunatic, a fanatic, a fool? Yes, he was all three – and that is why I think your Hasidic movement has succeeded. Am I right, Rabbi?"

"You are partly right, Mrs. Steiner. We have succeeded because of our *mesiras nefesh*, total commitment. But being zealous alone is not the answer. The Hasid knows the answer to the most important questions a person asks to achieve a happy and joyous life: What is his identity? What are his duties? What is his mission? Why was he born? Above all, he lives in a community that is loving, supportive and friendly where he can share his life. The Hasid is never lonely.

"But *The Lonely Crowd* epitomizes modern America and is its most profound spiritual and psychological pathology. We Lubavitchers are able to fill the great void in the hearts and souls of *The Lonely Crowd* with *Yiddishkeit* - joyous and positive ideals and practices of traditional Judaism. That is our mission and we have succeeded because we understand the true nature of modern society's pathology."

Freda listened carefully and responded, "I understand you, Rabbi, but I have a number of questions. You know that every medication, no matter how effective, often has a negative side effect."

"I'm listening."

"There is a negative side-effect to the Lubavitcher way of life. Do you mind if I offer criticism?"

"Please speak your mind honestly."

FREDA began, "In the past two hundred years, since the emancipation of the Jews in Europe, the Jewish people have made a profound impact in the advancement of science, the arts, music, medicine and law. What would the world be like without, great men like Albert Einstein, and hundreds like him? In America, Jews have become Presidents and Deans of prestigious colleges including Harvard and Princeton, schools that once excluded Jews. In fact, five of the eight Ivy League universities have a Jewish President!

"Children of immigrants have enriched our country and become the elite of American society. In the field of American music: George Gershwin, Richard Rogers, Jerome Kern, Irving Berlin and Leonard Bernstein are foremost. And the most esteemed folk-singers in the world are: Bob Dylan, Paul Simon, Art Garfunkel and Leonard Cohen.

"My family and I love American popular music and our lives have been enriched along with the rest of this country.

"I love Israel and I am an ardent life-long member of Hadassah. I'm proud to declare that my husband and I are the largest contributors to U.J.A. in Wiltonbury. As a matter of fact, Henrietta Szold and Golda Meir are my most inspiring heroes."

"What is your point, Freda?"

"It is obvious, Rabbi. Among all these great Jews cited, and I might add the names of Israel reborn: Herzl, Ben-Gurion, Meir, Weizmann, Eban, Rabin, and Begin – not one was Orthodox! What would have happened if these outstanding Jews were converted to the narrow Lubavitcher ideology? Your movement has not been pro-Zionist!

"Indeed, it was their integration and assimilation into modern Europe and America that enabled them to influence, transform and improved the Jewish people and the entire civilized world."

Rabbi Hecht said, "I admit that."

Freda continued, "Your movement boasts that thousands of your students avoid college and higher secular education to become, *Sheluchim*, Emissaries – blind to the cultural benefits of modernity. How can you be sure that in the rigorous and exclusive total immersion of Torah education you are also destroying their greater potential?"

RABBI HECHT replied, "You have a good point, Freda, except that the work of our Emissaries – to hasten the Messianic Era of universal peace and love - is more important! Let me remind you that science and technology produced Nazism, the greatest evil in human history and the Holocaust. Did you know that most of the fifteen Nazi officials that attended the Wannsee Conference in 1942 to plan the Holocaust were university graduates – and eight had Ph.D.'s?

"Does the world need more secular-scientific knowledge or Torah values? We believe that at the present time the spiritual work of our Emissaries will achieve a greater world. You marvel at the progress of the two hundred years of Emancipation and secular-scientific progress that also caused more deaths and misery in human history than the first five thousand years. Our spiritual mission is to hasten the coming of the Messiah and usher in universal peace, love and blissful happiness for all time."

FREDA responded, "I see your point, Rabbi, and I wish you and your religious educational endeavors continued success. You will receive a generous check from the Steiners Foundation. However, I believe that we are both right! Modern secular-scientific progress needs traditional religious values. I wish there were an effective synthesis of your total immersion in Torah studies and a program of secular-scientific studies. Am I correct in recalling my former Rabbi, who quoted from the Pirkei Avot: 'Beautiful is Torah study with *derech eretz,* practical work. Torah without practical work is worthless and leads to sin?'"

"You are correct, Freda, the key-word is *with*. But at this moment we give priority to Torah studies."

THE PASSING of sixty years witnessed dramatic changes in Wiltonbury, the dwindled Jewish community and Beth El Synagogue. Young men and women went off to college, but upon graduation, set their sights on larger and more vibrant cities. Freda had made numerous adjustments after her husband, Howard, passed away and she too was now spending six months in Florida.

She often met with some of her friends from Wiltonbury at Early Bird specials on Collins Avenue. But she enthusiastically supported the fund-raising affairs for her most passionate interests - the Yeshiva of Miami, Hadassah, Israel Bonds and her Beth El Synagogue.

Her friends would comment, "Where do you get your resilience, Freda, to be active in so many organizations? Isn't it time to retire the Lioness and enjoy the sunny and relaxed casual lifestyle of Florida?"

Freda would respond affirmatively, "This Lioness refuses to be caged."

The Steiners had sold their business and the ability to sustain the Beth El synagogue was in peril.

Most of the *machers* were deceased, or residents in Nursing Homes. Freda received an alarming call from Hershel Drinsky, the President of Beth El. It was a crisis!

"Freda, there is talk of selling the Beth El building to a church or even demolishing it for residential construction. What shall we do? The Board is divided."

"Don't panic, Hershel. This Lioness refuses to be caged. Hold on a few weeks."

Freda returned to Wiltonbury in the spring and she resumed her efforts, with a generous gift from the Steiners Foundation to preserve the ninety years old Beth El edifice.

HOW LOVE CAME TO REB LEIZER

Charles H. Freundlich

The Third Mountain

SEVEN YEARS after the establishment of the State of Israel, I was fortunate to receive a scholarship for a year's study in a Yeshiva in Jerusalem. I was twenty-one, recently graduated from college, and full of Zionist passion. For the past few weeks my mother and I had serious discussions and some heated arguments about my forthcoming trip to Israel – to be separated for a full year from family. My mother's anxiety was not only about my personal safety and a year's separation from family, but about the unsettling climate of war in the Middle East.

When the joyous day in June finally arrived for my departure on the S.S. Jerusalem, my mother accompanied me to the pier. As I ascended the steps to board the ship I could clearly see my mother's face. There were tears in her eyes. I had never seen my mother cry. She had always maintained a sense of strength and stoicism when she managed the family during crises and the challenging times of the Great Depression. My mother's tears were not of sorrow but of a deeply felt love for me which words could not convey.

My exuberant excitement for my year's program in Israel overwhelmed me for months but could not dim the powerful memory of sadness and love within me that was stirred by my mother's tears.

TIME passed quickly and my year's study was a great personal triumph and a transformative experience. I had matured, broadened my vision and expanded my knowledge. Above all, I had confronted the complex dimensions of my own soul and the mystery of love.

Most noteworthy was my study with Reb Leizer, a brilliant Talmudic scholar in Jerusalem who tutored me for my examinations for *Semicha,* ordination. Reb Leizer's deep commitment to Torah and his own personal and desperate search for love were to inspire and enlighten me for the rest of my life. I share this remarkable story of love with you, my dear reader.

WHEN REB LEIZER strolled down Rechov Yaffo, the main thoroughfare of Jerusalem in the morning, he was recognized by everyone. He wore the same shabby grey suit, wrinkled white shirt, loose-fitting tie, and a fedora that was in need of cleaning and reshaping. It was ten o'clock and it was time to purchase *The Jerusalem Post,* an English newspaper, which he was able to read effortlessly. Though he was hardly forty years old, his face was wrinkled and sallow. It gave the impression that the vibrant and energetic milieu of Israel reborn had passed him by. He personified a reincarnation of the old world - a denizen of a long-forgotten Lithuanian *shtetl,* a phantom that had risen from the grave.

"Poor Reb Leizer," the clerk mused, when he left the store, "he must be very lonely, without wife or family." Reb Leizer did not regard these unspoken sentiments, nor did he view himself in a pitiful or woeful condition. He was a *talmid chacham,* a Talmudic doyen, a *masmid,* a wholehearted devotee of Torah-study who resided within the walls of the famous Hebron Yeshiva for almost his entire life.

Who would have believed that this outstanding middle-aged, and unmarried member of the Hebron Yeshiva, was still living permanently in the student dormitory? He was not old, like the elders of the Yeshiva - just tired and distraught, bereft of youthful vitality, lacking a dream or ideal that could revitalize him. For the past twenty years, he hardly altered his daily regimen: morning *Minyan* services in the *Beth HaMidrash,* Study Hall, breakfast with the other students, then returning to his private room to read The Jerusalem Post and the numerous English books he had collected and stored, stacked in neat piles in the middle of his room. This schedule was completed in one hour.

Reb Leizer then attended to his numerous private students, mostly from America, in preparation for their examinations for *Semicha,* Orthodox ordination. Each tutorial lasted about forty-five minutes and the payment he received was in American dollars, which after many years was a considerable sum that was clandestine from the Yeshiva administration. Following the morning schedule, he returned to the Yeshiva for Talmud study in the large *Beth HaMidrash* with the other students for an hour which was followed by the main meal at midday consisting of brown bread, jelly, vegetable soup, fresh salad, fruit and tea.

Reb Leizer was accustomed to eat modestly in accordance with the ascetic discipline of his father who was a disciple of the *Mussar,* ethical movement. He partook of the vegetable soup, and one slice of dark bread with jelly.

After conversing with some of his fellow students, he ambled down the streets to escape the stuffiness of the Yeshiva. He would meander down Rechov Yaffo until the bottom of the hill before Ben Yehuda Street, and turn to Rav Kook Street. There he would enter a small, slovenly courtyard where two goats were loosely tied to a tree. He would feed them with pieces of bread which he had carried in his jacket pocket and contemplate this small quiet island of God's creation, isolated from the crowded and boisterous streets of Jerusalem's center.

In those moments of quiet isolation he would feel sheltered from the demeaning glares and sentiments of the narrow-minded denizens of the Yeshiva. Here, in this private space, alone with his friendly goats, he felt contented and peaceful. Was this not the presence of God?

But was he unnoticed from human eyes? He sometimes sensed that behind the curtains of the

---

---

windows in an adjacent antiquated stone building of the Turkish era, there were eyes that pierced his privacy and invaded his special domain. Were the curtains moving?

ONE of the older students tormented Leizer, "Why do you, a *Masmid,* who is privileged with a private room at the Yeshiva, and who converses with us in Yiddish, have to read the *goyishe* English Jerusalem Post?" Leizer would offer a sardonic smile, "It is my sacred secret." Other students speculated that he was secretly preparing to flee the narrow and constricting world of Orthodoxy and the Jerusalem Yeshiva and make a new life for himself in America, the land of promise and enlightenment. He heard that many of the rabbis and students of the Lithuanian Yeshiva world had emigrated to New York and New Jersey after World War II. Others speculated that Reb Leizer longed to be respected and recognized as a worldly scholar, and English fluency was the sine qua non in modern Israeli circles.

But these critics did not know nor could they fathom the secret yearnings in Reb Leizer's heart. He would offer a dismissive smile and walk away with indifference. It was none of their God damn business, he thought. What he desired most of all was to discover the knowledge and experience of true love, the romantic experience he read about in the numerous American novels he had accumulated.

WHEN Reb Leizer returned to his room, he would clutch the numerous volumes of modern American literature to his heart, hoping to discover the meaning of love from Ernest Hemingway, William Faulkner, John Steinbeck and Sinclair Lewis. He would kiss and embrace them as loving and dear comrades. These novels transported him to Paris, Spain, New York, and Oklahoma and would awaken his mind and stimulate the depths of his soul to escape from the cold and unfeeling isolation of the Yeshiva.

These were his moments that revealed the truth about the outside world - that life was grander, richer, and more exciting than the life of perpetual study of the outmoded arid texts of the Talmud. Life was too precious and wonderful to be wasted on the lifelessl path he had trodden during these past twenty years. My dear American authors, he mused, I love your tales of excitement, wonder and adventure. They are superior to the ancient texts of the Talmud. You are my dearest and devoted friends.

Charles H. Freundlich

LEIZER was not always an outlier from the other students of his famous Yeshiva. In fact, he was a pioneer, one of the first students who arrived at Hebron in 1924 with his parents and more than fifty other students from the Lithuanian Yeshivas Knesset Yisrael. They had fled from Slobodka, Lithuania, and settled in the ancient town of Hebron in colonial Palestine. Jews, they felt, were no longer welcome in the newly-reborn independent Lithuania. In the wake of the nationalist fever there, political sentiment had become hostile to other minorities, ethnic, and national groups, and especially towards the Jews. Earlier promises and assurances of granting national rights to Jews were disregarded. New harsh requirements of secular studies were demanded in the Yeshiva and its young students feared the possibility of being drafted into the military.

The departure from Slobodka, Lithuania was imperative. The relocation to Hebron, Palestine, was not motivated by Zionist aspirations, but pragmatic realities. Where else would Orthodox Jews be welcome? Jerusalem was deemed too conservative and archaic for the Lithuanian Yeshiva and Hebron, though populated with Arabs, was a more pragmatic option.

The Third Mountain

But the Arab uprisings of 1929 in Palestine, inflamed up by the Grand Mufti of Jerusalem, Haj Amin al-Husseini, caused the slaughter of sixty-seven Jews in Hebron including twenty-four yeshiva students. This horrific tragedy compelled the Yeshiva heads to relocate to the safety of Jerusalem where they settled in the old Geula neighborhood. Among those murdered were Leizer's parents. His father, Reb Nutte, a respected Talmudic scholar, had taught at the Yeshiva and Leizer, recently Bar Mitzvah, became the ward of the Rosh Yeshiva, the esteemed Reb Chatzkel Stern.

LEIZER vowed: *Tatteh,* I will devote every minute of my life to the Talmud as you have done and be an honor to your memory. Leizer upheld his father's legacy and became a *Masmid,* mastering both the Talmud and the four sections of the *Shulchan Aruch,* the official code of Jewish law, before his twentieth birthday. He was not only gifted in Talmud but was also endowed with handsome features and a vibrant and affable personality. He was open and available to all students in the large *Beth HaMidrash* who sought his assistance in explaining complex passages in the Talmud. Eventually, he acquired the status of a *Talmid Chacham,* a recognized master of the Talmud, and was selected by Reb Chatzkel to become an official expert tutor to the student novices who came from all over Israel, Europe and the United States to study in Jerusalem at the famous Hebron Yeshiva.

Leizer's future was bright and hopeful as he approached his twentieth birthday and contemplated marriage. As was the tradition, he approached Reb Chatzkel, to select a worthy mate, perhaps one of the daughters of the leading *Rabbis* of the Yeshiva.

LEIZER WOULD never forget that encounter with Reb Chatzkel following the morning Minyan, with the searing words emblazoned on his soul: "Of course, my dear Leizer, we shall select a proper mate for you. But to expect a daughter of one of the Roshei Yeshivas is out of the question."

Leizer was flustered, "Out of the question? I do not understand."

"My dear Leizer, I have treated you like my own son these past seven years. You are part of our family and we are proud of your learning and piety. You are truly a *Ben Torah* and *Talmid Chacham*, an exceptional product of the Hebron Yeshiva. But..."

"But - what?"

"I thought that your dear father, my dear colleague, Reb Nutte, of blessed memory, explained it to you. I mean how you came to be his son."

"I don't understand."

"Oy, vey. It was never explained. I would have thought that Reb Nutte explained all the details when you became a Bar Mitzvah. It is a most delicate subject and I shall have to divulge the tragic story now."

"Please tell me everything."

"Three years after your parents wedding they were informed by leading medical experts that they could never have children. Your dear mother, Chana, of blessed memory, an exemplary wife, and an *eishes chayil,* had undergone a serious and complicated pregnancy and in order to save her life a delicate operation on the fetus and other tissues were removed. Poor Chana almost bled to death. But the *Almighty* spared her life in the merit of your dear father, but was informed that she would not be able to have a child.

"About seven months later, in the middle of the night, a foundling baby was left at the door steps of the Yeshiva. The baby was crying. One of the *Masmidim,* who was still studying in the Beth HaMidrash, brought the baby to me. I knew that it was a sign from Heaven that your dear parents would have a child. That baby was you."

"And who were my real parents?" Leizer asked.

"We do not know. You were a foundling. You may have been born from a young unmarried Arab girl – perhaps an unmarried Jewish girl. We do not know and it is not important. You were circumcised and immersed in a *mikvah* for conversion and reared as an authentic Jew."

Leizer was distraught, "I understand. If born by an unknown mother, I am like a *shtuki,* one with questionable pedigree, and not fit to marry into one of the prestigious rabbinic families."

"Correct. It would not be fitting that one of our rabbinic daughters marry a man of defective pedigree – perhaps of a Gentile, or even a *mamzer,* bastard, from an adulterous married woman, who would contaminate the pure lineage of our Yeshiva Rabbis."

LEIZER would recall the words, *shtuki, mamzer, contaminate,* that were like a dagger in his heart. The piercing wound resonated in his thoughts every day during the past twenty years. Would he ever find love?

Reb Leizer pondered: What do these ignorant people know about my heart and dreams? I sacrificed my life for Torah-study exclusively. I did not attend the movies or join any social club, never wasted my time drinking coffee and smoking in the

Atara Café on Ben Yehuda Street like the Americans I tutor for ordination. I lived my life in my sacred world in my own way. I became a *Masmid* and by the time I was twenty I was a *Buki,* a master of the entire Talmud. Cite any quotation from the Talmud and I will indicate the *Masechta,* volume, the complex analysis and the primary rabbinical opinions. The elders of the Yeshiva lauded my brilliance and I was assigned to tutor the most gifted young foreign students with generous remunerations.

The Deans of the Yeshiva, arranged for other less erudite students to marry their daughters. Never me! I should have been their primary choice. I would then be granted a permanent appointment in the Yeshiva faculty. The hell with their hypocritical manners! The hell with their sympathy and their pathetic acts of pity!

AS A PERMANENT senior student of the Hebron Yeshiva, Reb Leizer received a modest monthly stipend, and the right to take his meals from the main dining room and eat privately in his room. Some students wondered: what was in that private room of Reb Leizer? Was it like the Holy of Holies, where he would commune directly with the angels of God?

Charles H. Freundlich

Reb Leizer had a reputation as an excellent tutor which attracted foreign students, mostly from America, to prepare for the examination to receive Semicha, ordination, from the famous Hebron Yeshiva. An ordination from the Hebron Yeshiva was universally esteemed comparable to a degree from Harvard.

In his long tenure at the Yeshiva, Reb Leizer had not only become a *Buki*, a master of the Talmud but also of the *Yoreh Deah*, the portion of the Code of Jewish law dealing with kosher laws which were the most significant requirement to receive Orthodox *Semicha*. An American Rabbinical student seeking a speedy and valid *Semicha* from Hebron was required to study at the yeshiva for about a year, to pay a modest monthly sum to a senior student, who served as his tutor and mentor, who in turn subsequently advised the Dean to grant an official Hebron Ordination diploma.

Reb Leizer reached out to other rabbinical students who did not attend Hebron and offered his services both as a tutor and guide for receiving alternate Ordination Certificates including from the prestigious Chief Rabbi of Israel.

American Rabbinical students heard, by word of mouth, about the expertise of Reb Leizer who charged a modest tutoring fee. Reb Leizer

146

understood the mentality of American rabbinical students; they wanted the ordination without the years of intensive study of the minutia of the other sections of the *Shulchan Aruch Code* which were not practical and irrelevant to America life

Reb Leizer shared the joy of his successful students who would return to America with a prestigious Hebron Ordination, find a lucrative pulpit, and a respected and honorable life. After all, these students were his children and he was their mentor.

Reb Leizer would not only teach his students the complex interpretations and the numerous commentaries of the Yoreh Deah for the examination, but he would also like to share with them and relate the details of the successful reports he received from his previous students in America.

Alas, Reb Leizer reflected: His students went on to lucrative careers as successful pulpit rabbis, chaplains and even as professors of Judaica in prestigious colleges. He treasured the air-mail letters from his students, his children, and even the photos of their families. They were enriched by him, but what did he have to show for his efforts other than a few hundred dollars with which he purchased classical American books and novels?

His numerous students respected Reb Leizer but they did not feel a strong, personal attachment. It was as if he lived in a separate domain behind a thick wall that could not be penetrated. They all wondered: how did a brilliant student of the Talmud end up a semi-recluse instead of a prime candidate for a daughter of one of the leading Hebron Rosh Ha-Yeshivas?

LEIZER PONDERED his dismal fate. He would die childless and unloved. Certainly he should have received the favor of God for his years of devoted study to His sacred books. Where had he gone astray? He prayed three times daily and observed all the minutia of the daily discipline prescribed by the *Shulchan Aruch*, the Orthodox code of law.

He was desperate and decided to pursue a radical scheme. He would turn to his American students who had experience and knowledge of real life. Perhaps, he could learn from them, and share their joyful experiences, which would open up a window for him to view life more fully. But how could he, a noted scholar, seek wisdom from his younger pupils? Was this not a shame, an admission of his failure? On the other hand, he must be courageous and begin a great transformation in his lifestyle.

BARRY FINKLE was one of his faithful students being tutored for ordination and he opened up his heart to him about his awful loneliness. Barry suggested that if he wanted some assistance in meeting women, he might have to make some radical changes.

One afternoon after tutoring Barry, he confessed his desperation to alter his present lonely way of life.

"I am asking you, Barry, for some help in my personal life."

Barry was nonplussed. Reb Leizer had never shared his personal feelings with his American students. They lived in a depraved hedonistic and immoral Gentile civilization that valued fun, material things and instant gratification. What did they have in common with this holy man, a spiritual, ascetic and unworldly scholar?

"I would be most happy to help you Reb Leizer if I were able. But what wisdom do I have that would be acceptable or useful to you?"

"I look at you Barry and I see a tall, handsome happy and very sociable person. When you smile, I suspect that many young and pretty girls are attracted to you. Am I right?"

"I think you are exaggerating though some of my friends consider me romantic and quite effective with girls."

"Then tell me, Barry, what must I do? I have no family, no children and no one who loves me."

"First, let me say, Reb Leizer that all your students admire and respect you."

"Respect – yes. But they do not love me!"

"Okay, if its love and romance you want let me make a few suggestions that can set you on the proper path which will lead to marriage."

"Of course, marriage."

"We can begin by choosing the right social activity – such as coffee together at the Atara Café where many young people gather in the afternoon and evening to socialize, chat, share stories, jokes and political opinion. If you want to be accepted as part of this social set, you must make a few important changes. First, we must change the way you appear. You must dress appropriately for modern social life. Get rid of your old hat – perhaps wear a beret. You need to wear a bright colored shirt and light-colored trousers. You might try wearing sandals instead of your shoes. In other words, you must dress stylishly like modern young people open to romance and love."

"Will you help me purchase these suitable clothes?"

"Naturally, but you will have to hide your new clothes from the Yeshiva. You can change in my apartment – keep your old clothes when you attend yeshiva, and change into your new fashionable clothes when we attend the café. "

"When do we begin?"

"Right now. We'll buy a new wardrobe and tomorrow we can meet at the Atara Café at 8:00 P.M.."

"God bless you, Barry. I already feel excited and optimistic."

WHEN Reb Leizer and Barry sat down at one of the tables on Ben Yehuda Street, there were at least twenty young people chatting, smoking and having coffee.

Barry pointed to a table with two young women and two empty chairs. "Those two women are not accompanied. It's a sign that they are open to new relationships. I'll ask them to join us." He approached the women.

"Shalom. I'm Barry. I noticed that you two beautiful women did not order yet. How about joining me and my friend Leizer for a cup of coffee and some fantastic conversation? It would be my pleasure to treat you."

"My name is Rachel. Dorit and I were supposed to meet a few friends, men, a half-hour ago. But they didn't show up. I suppose we can join you."

Barry smiled. "I hope you don't mind my imperfect Hebrew. I have been in Israel for only six months. But I studied Hebrew in High School."

"That's fine with us," said Rachel. "We both studied English for four years in High School. You know, most Israelis can speak English and we can chat in English."

"We are delighted just to be with you. My friend Leizer speaks fluent Hebrew."

Leizer was observing Dorit. She was beautiful. He beheld her dark hair, her glistening eyes, her pink lips, and her tan smooth complexion. Her breasts were well-shaped, no doubt, a Sabra. He could feel a stirring sensation within and a slight palpitation in his chest. Was this love?

"What do you both do when you're not at the Atara Café?" Dorit asked.

Leizer smiled and responded, "I'm a lecturer in Talmud and Codes and I tutor foreign students seeking ordination in Israel."

"That sounds fascinating. You must meet a lot of interesting people," Dorit added.

"Barry, here, is one of my students. He's from Antwerp, Belgium."

"Belgium? Is your family in the Diamond business? I hear that Jews control the international Diamond trade in Europe," Rachel said.

"My family and many of my relatives are in the Diamond business, but most Jews are merchants and shop-keepers. They are not all rich as the anti-Semites assert."

"And what do you two beautiful women do when you are not socializing at the Atara Café?" Barry asked.

"We are both students at the Hebrew University, Dorit said. "We both are studying political science. Hopefully, we will have a career in the Foreign Service. You know that Israel has formed diplomatic branches in many African countries."

After an hour, the conversation was tiring

"Dorit said, "I think it's time for us to leave. We have a very long and difficult program tomorrow."

"Leaving so soon?" Barry asked.

Dorit said, "We enjoyed meeting you both and engaging in interesting conversation. We are grateful for your treating us to coffee. But, perhaps we can meet again at another time?"

"We were delighted to meet you," Barry responded. "We both look forward to meeting you again."

WHEN the girls left, Leizer asked, "Well, did we succeed in making new friends. I thought Dorit was very pretty."

"I'm afraid we did not make a great impression. If they were interested in us they would have given us their address or phone numbers. But you never can tell after a first encounter."

"Frankly, I found it very audacious to approach strange girls," Leizer declared. "I'm sorry that it did not work out. I thought Dorit was very warm and friendly."

"It's part of the game," Barry responded. "People come to a cafe in the evening with an open mind willing to meet new faces. Anyway, in Israel all Jews are family."

"What do we do next?" Leizer asked.

"We can attend a singles social at the community center. Do you mind dancing with a woman?"

"Heaven forbid!" Leizer responded.

"Them we would be better off going to Tel Aviv and can attend a modern Zionist social group, the *Mishmeret Tseirah,* where they have mixed folk dancing."

"That sounds more reasonable."

IT WAS serendipity, Dorit had just broken up with her boyfriend. She was distraught and was pleased that Leizer and Barry had invited her and Rachel to their table.

"What did you think of Barry and Leizer?" Dorit asked Rachel.

"I thought Barry was nice, but he was too young for me. Leizer was interesting but kind of old."

"I think that older guys make good husbands. They are more experienced," Dorit said.

"Do you think that we should have given them our address?"

"Perhaps," said Dorit.

LEIZER was confused. "I felt that Dorit was very beautiful. I felt my heart beating. Was that a sign of love?"

Barry responded, "Perhaps it was romantic love. You have to realize, Leizer, that there are all kinds of love: Motherly love that is unconditional, fatherly love that is conditional like friendship and your love for God that is purely spiritual. Romantic love is a kind of mystery. It can't be explained - only experienced. It is caused by hidden triggers hormones, and chemicals in your body, that propel you to feel a powerful sense of oneness with another person. Be careful of romantic love which is not the best road to a happy marriage. People that fall in love and marry because of Romantic love easily fall out of love. Of course, Romantic love caused by your hidden desires and chemistry is the beginning of a love that matures over time and leads to marriage. Mature love must be based on a meeting of minds, dreams and values."

"I think I will try to meet with Dorit once again and find out about her religious life, her ideals and dreams."

WHEN I met with Barry and Reb Leizer a few days later, he discussed his experience at the Atara Café and his meeting with Dorit. "What did I think about love?" Leizer asked.

"I told him that the basis of all love is self-sacrifice or giving fully of yourself to another person, cause or God."

"That is all? Reb Leizer asked.

"No, that is the beginning. What happens after self-sacrifice is the merging of your soul with another person. When your two souls are one, then you are in love."

"But how will I know if my soul is merged with another person?" Reb Leizer asked.

I answered, "That is the magic of love. You and the person you love will feel a joy within that is indescribable with words but clearly known in your heart. And when you are separated, you will feel tears in your eyes."

REB LEIZER contacted Dorit and they met at the Atara and other cafes, for three months. Eventually she invited Reb Leizer to her home to meet her parents. Her father, a biblical scholar, admired Reb Leizer and Dorit was delighted that she received his approval.

TWO MONTHS later, I returned to New York, having successfully passed all my exams to be ordained by the Chief Rabbi. I was most indebted to Reb Leizer for his masterful tutoring and promised to write him regularly. Barry had left Israel and would return to America to finish his college studies before returning permanently to his family in Antwerp.

Charles H. Freundlich

ABOUT six months later, Barry wrote me from Antwerp about the further events of Reb Leizer's quest for love.

"You won't believe it, but Reb Leizer has married Dorit. They are expecting their first child."

I felt tears in my eyes - tears of love.

THE THIRD MOUNTAIN

Charles H. Freundlich

The Third Mountain

IT WAS A WARM and sunny day in Miami Beach and the blue sky had barely any clouds. Numerous tourists were strolling on the boardwalk. I was sitting on a bench and chatting with Dr. Jeremy Lauer, an old friend and a fellow high school alumnus. The sounds of waves cresting to the beach broke the peaceful silence.

"Listen, Jeremy, I asked to meet you here, away from your home and office, so that we can talk in strict privacy. I haven't discussed my problem with my wife and did not want to meet you in your office where your wife might see me and ask about my personal life."

Jeremy replied, "First, let me say that it's always a delight to meet with you. And second, we both agree that Miami Beach is the closest depiction of our vision of Paradise – right? So what can be wrong as we leisurely lounge in the warmth of the sun? I guess I take the warm and soothing weather for granted having lived here for twenty years.

"You should know that as a professional psychiatrist, any conversations between us are confidential. Too bad, we haven't got together more often socially during the past few years. Anyway, I decided not to retire – I could use the extra fees to help support my grandchildren. They haven't found themselves yet. But that's another story. What's bothering you? Why, the secrecy?"

"I'm not sure, Jeremy. That's why I wanted to talk to you. We've known each other for more than sixty years since our high school days. I know that I can speak to you freely and with utmost confidentiality. However this is the first time I am seeking your advice as a psychiatrist and not as a loyal friend."

"I'm a professional, and whatever we discuss remains private and confidential."

The Third Mountain

I REFLECTED for a moment: I had known Jeremy practically all my life. We both commuted to school from the Bronx and we spent many hours discussing school work, Zionism, dating, sports, and current events. We both were children of Yiddish - speaking immigrants and we shared the American dream of success through education.

Jeremy had a fantastic mind, was well-read and many considered him to be the top student in our class. He would continue being an elite student after completing college and Yale Medical School. His fulfillment of the American ideal seemed almost flawless. But he had one physical drawback. He was not good-looking and his skin color was sallow. Needless to say, he was very self-conscious, had a challenging social life, and difficulty finding a suitable wife. He was overly sensitive about his looks and felt insecure when dating. Perhaps that is why he took an interest in psychology and chose to become a psychiatrist.

Since our graduation from high school, Jeremy and I kept in touch and we had much to share. We both spent a year in a study-program in Israel after we graduated from college and shared a passionate love for both Hebrew and Yiddish Literature. After we both married and raised our kids, our relationship diminished to exchanging greeting cards at the High Holiday season.

I CONTINUED, "Let me get to the heart of the problem."

"You don't have to rush things," Jeremy responded. "I have no other appointments this morning. I thought we would chat and do lunch together like the old times."

"Okay for lunch."

EVER since I graduated college and stopped playing varsity basketball, I began gaining weight. Just looking at a piece of layer cake near my plate increases my weight. It seems that I have been devoting half of my life to losing weight and staying trim for a year or two to play racquetball and tennis

"I must admit that you look quite athletic for an eighty-year old," Jeremy said, as he dug into his Eggplant Parmesan.

Jeremy was slightly overweight with a visible paunch but he had no health concerns. He devoured his entree and completed his dessert, a Chocolate Éclair, with great relish. I ordered a tuna-salad sandwich and fresh fruit.

"Jeremy, here's the problem. I am severely depressed. Since I completed my last book of fiction, and received mixed reviews, I haven't written anything. It's as if my life was over and I had nothing more to say or contribute. I don't dream or feel a sense of excitement or purpose. I feel tired as if my entire creativity was drained. I lack passion to do anything. Worst of all, I haven't been able to sleep. I feel like a wreck."

"You don't sound like the friend I knew all my life. You were a star athlete and I understand that you still play a wicked game of racquetball twice a week. How long have you felt this way?"

I continued, "I reached this crisis in my life about five months ago. I suppose my depression is not life-threatening. Suicide does not enter my mind, thank God. But my depression is formidable enough to stir up and awaken many buried experiences and traumas of my youth. I overcame my early depressions by directing my thoughts to the future. I dreamed great and passionate dreams, and fulfilled many of them.

"But suddenly my past has overtaken me. I constantly think about some of my unfortunate and unhappy experiences growing up in the Bronx - the numerous times I did not have decent clothes or money for the movies and other things. I thought I had vanquished the tragic incidents of my early years.

"When I wrote my first novel about growing up in the Bronx, I had to recall those numerous sorrowful chapters reliving the pain buried deep in my memory. But having awakened my past, I feel I have retrogressed and am still living in the past. My past now dominates my daily thoughts. I know that it sounds crazy, but I felt that I had to speak to someone who understands and cares about me. You have been my most trusted friend."

Jeremy listened with attentiveness and responded, "This sounds like one of our many discussions when we were both in our twenties. We were at the crossroads of our lives, still troubled, confused, unsettled, unmarried and beginning our careers. How well I remember those long and heated discussions in Crotona Park about everything and nothing. It was very comforting and uplifting just hearing your views which were mostly contrary to my own. Nevertheless we both benefitted from our discussions. So, what's new?"

"Let me put it succinctly. I am now in my eighties, like you, and living in Florida since my retirement with my wife, Honey, of fifty-six years, and she is now facing serious health issues. It was time to prepare for our inevitable ending by reviewing our wills and choosing a cemetery for purchasing grave plots. But - where?

"Both of our parents and several relatives were buried in Long Island, the site of most of the cemeteries that serviced the Jewish population of New York City. We still make an annual trip to New Montefiore Cemetery before the holiday season when we travel north to visit our children and grandchildren. The matter should have been simple. We would be buried near our parents."

"Okay," Jeremy responded, "but what's the crisis? Naturally you want to be buried in a place which has some significance to you and with which you are familiar. Your kids can visit you and Honey and even your parents' graves."

I explained, "I understand. But what precipitated the crisis was a notice I received from my shul a month earlier regarding the sale of gravesites in Beth HaChaim Cemetery outside Jerusalem. Many of my fellow congregants announced their desire to be buried in Israel. The cost was much higher than in the United States, but they felt it was worth it. It was the cherished dream of generations of religious Jews to be buried in Israel, especially in Jerusalem."

"I'm listening."

"Honey and I have been fervent Zionists since our youth and visited Israel numerous times. We viewed Israel as our spiritual home and felt energized and uplifted after each visit. But burial in Israel never crossed our minds. We cherished each trip to Israel but knew in our hearts that we would return to America because our children and grandchildren were living near New York. They would, no doubt, want our graves to be accessible to them."

JEREMY responded, "It seems to me, you are worrying about a trivial problem, not a crisis. Your choice of a gravesite should be comforting to you, not to your children. Can you be sure where your own children will be buried? Suppose they move to California. Will they make an annual trip to Long Island or to Jerusalem? I think you should resolve your indecision based on your own preference, and not your children's future convenience. It's that simple. My wife and I have decided to be buried in Miami, although our children still live up North. Visiting our graves is their problem, not ours. Though Dotty and I have very strong feelings for Israel, we are Americans. Remember that I studied in Israel, like you, right after college and was transformed, but still recognized that my home is here in America."

"I always admired your clear thinking, Jeremy. Perhaps you are right. Our decision is not a crisis. It simply is a difficult choice to make."

Jeremy smiled, "I'm glad we got together. Somehow life seems to have passed so quickly. I remember when we used to run to the park between classes to play basketball. Those were great days."

"JEREMY, I still feel a little unsettled. I suspect that this matter regarding burial is the tip of another more profound dilemma in my life."

"I know what you are thinking. You sense that your life is coming to an end. Half of our classmates are dead and the other half are in Nursing Homes or are struggling with their handicaps and walking with canes or walkers. You want to know the answer to the most important questions: Did you live fully? Will you leave a legacy to be remembered?"

"I think that you hit the nail on its head, Jeremy. I suspect that I was trying to avoid those questions for many years because they are very unsettling. Somehow I feel that I should have done more, worked harder, given more to my kids and to the community."

"Don't be so hard on yourself. I think you led an exemplary life – married to a lovely girl, had four beautiful children and had a successful career as a rabbi for fifty years. It's most remarkable that at age eighty you began writing fiction and published five excellent books. You invested your pension funds well and you and Honey are living a comfortable retirement in Florida. The only dream you and I never fulfilled was making Aliyah. After our first study-program in Israel, that was the central dilemma over which we agonized. We were in our twenties, unmarried, and had the potential to make the great move. But we both, despite our deep feeling for Israel and Zionism, chose not to make Aliyah. Aside from that, what more was lacking in your life?"

"That's what I want to know. Somehow I feel a recurrent emptiness in the portrait of my life. Something is missing. I just don't know what."

"There you go again, typical Jewish self-criticism. You know what? You might be better off talking to a rabbi?"

"I don't feel mentally disturbed, just dissatisfied. I feel I have to discover that missing feature, idea or feeling that will satisfy the hunger in my soul for a sense of completion and satisfaction. Am I asking too much from life?"

"No, I think your self-inquiry is legitimate. Most of us go through this period and try to change our course in life. Did you ever hear about mid-life crisis?"

"Jeremy, I went through a mid-life crisis forty years ago, and made dramatic changes. I feel I am past that stage."

"Perhaps it is something totally new. I believe it was David Brooks, who recently authored a book, about the need for personal transformation after successful people have realized most of their youthful dreams and become bored and filled with ennui. These successful people, who spent their lives struggling and straining to achieve celebrity and personal fulfillment, come to the realization, after a tragedy or traumatic event, that there is more to life. Something is missing. They have to begin a new lifestyle which Brooks calls *The Second Mountain*.

"This Second Mountain path is less interested in ego fulfillment or personal success. Rather it's a life of love, inter-dependence, service, a committed mission, and close relationships. This new lifestyle would initiate a special permanent, luminous joy that surpasses normal happiness. Most important, this lifestyle which is based on close relationships would ameliorate the current epidemic of suicides, alienation, divorce, opioids and loneliness.

"He argues that hyper-individualism and the quest for personal fulfillment, have caused modern society to become fragmented, dysfunctional and lonely. The four components of The Second Mountain are: Faith (Religion), Family (loving marriage), Vocation (committed mission) and Community. The ideology of *Hyper-Individualism* would be replaced by *Relationism*. What do you think?"

"Jeremy, I climbed my Second Mountain when I reached my eightieth birthday and I realized that my time was limited in bequeathing a long-lasting legacy. I began writing fictional stories based on my youth and rabbinical experiences. That was my committed mission or vocation. I crafted five books in five years. The purpose of these books was to record a personal testimonial - the saga of the vibrant, immigrant Jewish community of the Bronx that produced the building of beautiful synagogues, a dynamic religious life and a flourishing Yiddish culture. Their children, a new generation of inspired and educated American-Jewish youth, became the vanguard of their age in academia, science, technology, the arts, and business, including a number of Nobel Prizes laureates.

"This immigrant-Jewish society that flourished, declined and disappeared with the new waves of ethnic immigrants and the exodus of Jews to suburbia. My books are a historic record and testament to that splendid era of Jewish life in the Bronx for generations to come. That is my contribution and artistic legacy for my children, grandchildren and Jewish society. I felt it my mission to write these books as a service to the Jewish communities of the future.

"My married life with Honey continues to be joyous, and my children remain close and connected. I maintain a fruitful and creative connection to my shul and community. In short, I fulfilled the four pillars of the Second Mountain. So, why do I still feel distraught?"

Jeremy responded, "Superb. You claim you have climbed your Second Mountain successfully during these past five years. I see that you appear healthy, vibrant and dynamic. You wonder why you haven't achieved the promised resplendent joy. You wonder why you feel unfulfilled, having climbed the Second Mountain."

"The answer is obvious, Jeremy – The Second Mountain journey did not work for me. In fact, it does not work for most people. Let me give you another example of the failure of the Second Mountain.

"Remember Anna Goldberg? She used to live on Bryant Avenue when we both lived in the Bronx?"

"Was she that heavy blonde girl, the oldest of five children who was gung-ho about making Aliyah?"

"That was Anna. She was a deeply committed member of the Mizracha branch of Shomer HaDati that met near Crotona Park."

"I recall those days of fervent idealism and spirited Zionist activity very well. What about her?"

"Well, when she graduated from James Monroe High School she told her parents that she wanted to make Aliyah on a religious kibbutz. Naturally, they were opposed. They insisted that she finish college first. She agreed. After finishing college, she worked as a teacher for a year, contributed some money to the family, and then declared her intent to make Aliyah.

"Her father was upset because, as the oldest of the five children, her contribution of her salary to help with the monthly expenses was needed. Her father made a modest salary, but it was hardly enough to feed seven mouths. Nevertheless, she refused to set aside her idealism and dream. She made Aliyah and settled at a religious kibbutz. There she met David, also a Bronx boy who made Aliyah. They married and had two children. After five years, she and David realized that they were not happy with life on the kibbutz. They returned to America with some financial assistance from David's family and resumed their life as Hebrew teachers in Philadelphia."

"What's the point you are trying to make?"

"Don't you see? Anna was living on The Second Mountain and was unhappy! She had a profound Orthodox Jewish faith, a happy and loving family, a fervent belief in Zionism and Israel and a warm and friendly relationship within the kibbutz community and its ideology."

"So what went wrong?"

"She did not achieve that special feeling of *personal success*, status and recognition. She realized that the group, the collective, is more important and left no room for her personal self-esteem. And that is what is wrong with The Second Mountain. It assumes that one can achieve great joy by being totally altruistic and charitable and dedicated to the needs of others - the poor, the sick and the needy. The unselfish and ascetic life of the committed social justice warrior is unlikely to provide a luminous joy to anyone."

Jeremy suggested, "In that case, I would love to hear your critical analysis of Brooks' respected and admired work. Perhaps you could call it, *The Third Mountain*?"

"A *Third Mountain*? What do you mean? I haven't thought about a new book for the past five months. What could I write about today that I haven't written in my last five books?"

"I suspect you could write about your own failure to achieve the luminous joy promised by the author of *The Second Mountain*. Perhaps you need a change in venue. Florida is a dull and serene dumping ground for old people until they die. It is restful but not stimulating. You are too vivacious and can accomplish much more. You are not ready to retire from creative living.

"Forget about the gravesites for a moment and begin a new project: perhaps painting, in which you were trained in early age, or write a new sexy book or a play or take up the guitar and become a cantor. That's what you need - something new, bold and challenging to fire your soul and change the world."

"Thanks, Jeremy, for the encouragement. But I think your first suggestion is best for me. I should write a critical analysis of my failure to find permanent joy on the Second Mountain. I am too old to make a radical, transformative change. Perhaps I just need to make a modest adjustment, a change of venue, take a short trip, a journey into the deep caverns of my soul. This will be my ascent to *The*

Third Mountain, which will divulge the failures of The Second Mountain."

"Deep caverns of your soul? That sounds terrific, exciting and sensational. Can I tag along?"

"No, Jeremy. This is something too personal. What I was thinking about was writing a journal of a life that I still haven't lived. By retracing the major decisions I made when I reached a crossroad in my life and career and asked: What if I had made a different choice? What would have been my destiny in marriage and career?"

"That sounds great. Looking back and making an accounting of your life will no doubt give you a better perspective of where you were and where you want to be. What's your first step?"

"I think Honey and I will take a series of small trips to the places where I worked during the past fifty years. I would .like to meet some of the old faces – my congregants, and visit the shuls, perhaps worship there. That should be interesting and refreshing. I will now see my life in these former communities not as a young energetic rabbi, but as an experienced sage with a more nuanced and developed perspective. In other words, I will retrace my early life in former communities and observe it today from a contemporary viewpoint."

"I'm not sure I understand. You can't go home again. You know that. The past is gone. In my line of work, we visit the past in order to dredge up the mud and scars that contaminate and cripple our souls. No, you can't relive the past and simply say goodbye."

"Jeremy, you are too much of a realist. You forget that I have written five books recently about my earlier experiences. What was I doing? I was using the technique of the creative writer who returns to his past, and changes it to fit his desired ending. In creative writing, you *can go home again*!"

"Listen, I am a psychiatrist and delving into your past is part of my therapy. But recalling your past is used only to purge your neurosis and bring understanding and peace to your present. You live in the present not in the past."

"Not for the creative writer, Jeremy. The past and the present are fused into a unified time dimension. I think that my Third Mountain will be the creation that is planted in the depths of my soul and must be awakened. This climb will not be upward, but inward. Yes, I feel excited right now.

"I'll work out the basics during the next three months during my short journeys to my past, and then we'll get together for lunch to view my discoveries. This book will be called: *The Third*

Mountain, a journey of self-discovery that exposes the failure of The Second Mountain."

THE SECOND MEETING

Jeremy began, "It's wonderful to see you again looking so joyous. You looked like you were in the doldrums last time we met for lunch a few months ago."

"I really feel great, Jeremy. No, I feel joyous and jubilant. Here is a twenty page outline of *The Third Mountain.* Let me summarize the ideas for you here and you can read the detailed script later on."

"I am delighted to see you in good spirits. You know that three months ago when you were in your deep depression, I feared that you would grasp at a quick solution, a fad or a guru to give you instant relief. I'm glad you didn't fall into that trap that many others fall into in desperation, to find immediate relief. Anyway, let's eat first. I love the Israeli food they serve here. What about you?"

"I feel the same as you. Somehow, eating at this café brings back so many wonderful memories of my visits to Israel."

"Okay. Let's get down to basics. What did your journey on the Third Mountain achieve? Have you discovered the source of your former distress and sadness?"

"Yes, I have. What I discovered was that there was *no* Third Mountain. I returned to revise my evaluation of the Second Mountain which I previously thought sound and correct. Let me explain two fundamental ideas that I see as the flaws in The Second Mountain: First, the source of faith in God and religion; and second, the failure of so-called *Relationism*."

"I'm listening. I assume that you don't put much credence in mystical experiences as the source of the religious committed life."

"Correct. It's true that there are a number of famous people who claim to have been inspired by a personal mystical experience, a transcendent moment. But Judaism is a faith for the common man, not only for the saint or martyr. The biblical verse, *It is not in heaven* teaches that Judaism is practical and pragmatic within the grasp of the common man not an elitist way of life. Rabbi Samson Raphael Hirsch put it in these four Hebrew words, *Torah im Derech Eretz*. Torah (religion) must be combined with practical reality."

Jeremy probed, "What about the inspiring life of Jesus and the wonderful ideas in the *Beatitudes?* Are they not a splendid guide for all people in quest of a committed holy life? Would not Christianity be an alternate ideology?"

"Yes and no. Let me cite the work of Professor Joseph Klausner, of The Hebrew University, who wrote a number of outstanding studies about Jesus and Paul. The professor, an ardent Jew and Zionist, admired Jesus as perhaps the greatest of rabbis. But he laments the fact that Jesus' ideals and faith of total love, charity and unselfishness were too extreme for the common man and therefore it failed. Only martyrs, priests, saints and monks – cut off from the harsh realities of daily life - could fulfill the ideals of Jesus. Judaism was not to be the exclusive endeavor of a select few."

"How then, without mystical moments of transcendence, would the common man and woman attain faith in God?" Jeremy asked.

"The answer, Jeremy, is in the magic of daily *mitzvot,* duties, which are repetitive. For instance, Prayer is a daily mitzvah or duty. When you pray you follow the well-known principle of acting *as if.* To pray is to offer words to God *as if* God were present and listening. The repetition of *as if* prayer generates an indelible attribute on both the body and soul. The Jew who prays daily *becomes* a prayer! The Jew at prayer engages God *as if* they were bonded and united as one."

"It sounds reasonable. But how has this solved your problem of being distraught? You always offered daily prayer with *tefillin.*"

"I MUST CONFESS that my prayers were mechanical and rushed. At daily Morning Minyan we have to complete more that forty pages of prayers in a half-hour. There is hardly any time for being fully emotionally or consciously engaged. There was no *as if* God were before me, despite the words on the Ark in front of the synagogue: *I have placed the Lord before me always.* I've corrected it.

"I now pray better, slower and with more mindfulness. One does not need a mystical experience of transcendence to feel the presence of God. The gift of transcendence and prophecy were given to the few. But it is interesting that most of these few who were selected to experience the transcendent God: Abraham, Isaac, Jacob, Moses, and Amos, were common shepherds, not priestly elites.

"With all due respect to Maimonides - who believed that prophecy was vouchsafed to a select few who achieved an extraordinary level of intelligence and wisdom - the biblical prophets do not exhibit this endowment.

"Judaism permits the common man to achieve faith and spirituality without a martyr's pursuit to give away all his wealth to others, or to love all people unconditionally, or to neglect his own personal ego needs for wealth, success, status, honor and happiness."

JEREMY responded, "So you disagree with the author of The Second Mountain who asserts that our present society is hyper ego-centric, selfish, seeking self-actualization, success and personal fulfillment – all of which have led to loneliness, social decay, divorce, pessimism and suicide, - unlike previous generations which stressed interdependence, family, cooperation, altruism, community, charity and faith."

"Yes, I disagree. It is true that society has changed much but human nature has not. One cannot extend love to others without achieving self-love. One cannot be charitable without achieving personal financial success. One cannot be inter-dependent before becoming independent. In other words, you cannot give away anything unless you attain an abundance of that entity.

"Numerous self-driven, highly successful entrepreneurs, Titans of business, driven by the love of money, status and fame: Rothschild, Carnegie,

Rockefeller, Rosenwald, Gates, Buffett, and Bloomberg, became philanthropists and the financers of significant charitable foundations which endowed hospitals, universities, clinics, schools and research centers, which advanced human progress, freedom, liberty and happiness. These philanthropists often gave of their abundance for honor and recognition – with their names on college buildings, hospital wings or bronze plaques - which would enhance their celebrity, name and even immortality.

"Visit the amazing Hadassah Medical Center in Jerusalem which serves both Jews and Arabs, and note the numerous walls filled with names of donors on plaques. This great institution of philanthropy was financed by fund-raisers and others who understood the profound need in wealthy people to achieve fame and personal recognition.

"One did not have to become an ascetic, altruistic, totally dedicated and committed martyr in an impoverished African jungle, in order to benefit humanity. In fact, the Talmud asserts that the ascetic Nazirite must offer a sin-offering at the termination of his vow because he denied himself a legitimate pleasure of life - wine.

"Thus two of the pillars of the Second Mountain – a self-deprecating loyalty of faith and total commitment to a mission or cause are unrealistic and utopian. In addition, the call to abandon personal success and self-actualization for interdependence and relationships is inhuman and destructive.

"People who attain personal success and are self-actualized often become: the best of friends, husbands and wives, parents and neighbors and positive members of the community. People who neglect and deny their own personal ego needs and sense of success, recognition, and achievement - are incomplete and defective. They are often pessimistic and depressed and can hardly make positive contributions to society.

"Consider a champion basketball team. The culture of the sport is winning - not cooperation or sharing. The high-scorer of the team is often ego-driven which enables his team to win; but especially satisfies his ravenous personal need for recognition and status as a *Star* that may lead to an immense salary.

"Society recognizes and rewards individual merit, excellence and achievement far more than modesty and cooperative effort. A totally cooperative team-player who scores no points receives little celebrity. In sum: The use of disparaging words like: hyper-individualism and narcissism should refer to individuals who harm other people and society - not to be confused with true individualists who improve society.

"I believe that the source of many current social pathologies – loneliness, opioids, suicide and marital conflict - are symptoms of hyper-secularism which has destroyed traditional family values and sexual boundaries rooted in the Judeo-Christian religion. I note that most Orthodox Jewish families are happy, fruitful and triumphant – immune and insulated from these social pathologies."

JEREMY probed, "Then what have you concluded after three months of your personal journey? Do we need a Second Mountain to find luminous joy?"

"No. First lesson: Modern history has demonstrated that America, a free-market meritocracy upholding individualism, has promoted more liberty, prosperity and happiness than any nation founded on collective-socialism. Individualism is not a curse and is not *hyper*. Rather it is the engine for prosperity and happiness.

"Second lesson: A happy and joyous life cannot remain permanently on the peak of a mountain. Falling into a valley of despair or bad luck occasionally is only normal and part of the cycle of nature. It should stimulate your return to the top with courage and faith. A fall from the top may engender a period of sadness, as I experienced, but it does not require a radical change, only a review of the values and experiences that enabled my first successful journey to the peak.

"Mt. Sinai is our people's primary Mountain, and my true and tested road map for my next joyous journey."

JEREMY smiled, "I've listened very intently to your story, both as a psychiatrist and a long-time friend. I feel exhilarated from tagging along on your incredible and amazing trip. Bon Voyage and *L'hitraot,* my dear friend."

Charles H. Freundlich

ABOUT THE AUTHOR

CHARLES H. FREUNDLICH, the son of Gussie (Rindner) and Leon Freundlich, was born and raised in the Bronx, New York. His parents were immigrants from Eastern Galicia, part of the Austro-Hungarian Empire, now Ukraine. They taught him, by example, the three most important principles for the good life – Love, Work and Service.

He began his Jewish education in the Hebrew School of K'hal Adath Yeshurun, on Bryant Ave.

Charles H. Freundlich

Graduating P.S. 66 at the top of his class, he continued at Yeshiva Rabbeinu Chaim Ozer where he was the Valedictorian upon graduation. In Talmudical Academy High School he excelled in basketball, and graduated as a member of the Arista. After two years at Yeshiva College, he continued at Brooklyn College where he received his B.A., and from Yeshiva University's Bernard Revel Graduate School with an M.A. and a Doctor of Hebrew Literature.

He also studied at Mesivta Rabbi Chaim Berlin in Brooklyn and at Yeshivat Mercaz HaRav in Jerusalem, where he was ordained by Israel's Chief Rabbi, Isaac Halevy Herzog. He furthered his graduate work in Jewish studies at Columbia University and Dropsie College.

He served as Educational Director in New Bedford, MA and held rabbinic posts in Johnstown, PA, Norfolk, VA, Waterbury, CT, Pelham Parkway, Toronto and Delray Beach, FL.

After delivering sermons and lectures for fifty years he began writing fiction at age eighty, based on his incredible experiences.

Previous works include: Peretz Smolenskin: His Life and Thought, Vyse Avenue, Awake the Dawn, Sweet Is the Light, A Crown of Beauty, and

A Cup of Gladness. His numerous book-reviews and articles appeared in The Jewish Press.

He is married to the beautiful Deborah (Schmerler) and was blessed with four wonderful children: Judith, Sharon, Samson and Jessica and five precious grandchildren: Beverly, Isaac, Joshua, Elana and Adira.

He makes his home in Boca Raton, FL